# Still Yours, Always Mine

Tia Marlee

A NOVEL CHOICE

A Novel Choice Press

# Contents

To all the men and women who risk their lives every day to ensure the safety of others. Thank you!

# Annie

THE MOMENT I HEAR the name "Jake Colton" whispered through my bakery, I nearly drop an entire tray of blackberry scones.

"Did you hear?" Mrs. Fulton leans over the glass case, her voice carrying far more than she thinks it does. "The new fire chief is Tommy Colton's boy. Jake. The one who ran off all those years ago."

"Oh, I heard." Doris Simpson nods, eyes darting my way and then quickly back to her coffee. "Back with a teenager, too."

I keep my face neutral as I slide the tray into place. Twenty years of small-town living has taught me how to wear a mask, how to keep my hands steady when the rest of me wants to shake apart.

"Annie, honey," Mrs. Fulton calls, "did you hear about—"

"The new fire chief? Yes, ma'am." I wipe my hands on my apron, grateful for the flour dust that hides how pale my knuckles have gone. "Firelight Falls is lucky to have someone with big city experience."

What I don't say is that Jake Colton broke my heart when I was twenty-two years old. He left without a goodbye. And I've spent twenty years pretending I'm over it.

"Well, I think it's just wonderful," Mrs. Simpson says. "His poor mother needs him, what with her hip and all. And that girl of his needs some stability after losing her mother."

I nod, smile, and excuse myself to the kitchen where I can breathe.

Lana's there, elbow-deep in pie dough, her dark curls barely contained by her bandana. She takes one look at my face and says, "Spill it."

"Jake's back," I say, the words still feeling foreign on my tongue.

Lana stops kneading. "Jake Jake? As in—"

"First kiss, best friend, disappeared without a trace, Jake." I grab a rolling pin because I need something solid in my hands. "New fire chief Jake."

"Oh my goodness." Lana wipes her hands. "Are you okay?"

"I'm fine." The lie comes automatically. "It's been twenty years. Ancient history."

"Uh-huh." Lana crosses her arms. "And that's why you look like you've seen a ghost."

"I'm just surprised," I say, rolling out dough with more force than necessary. "It's a Tuesday. Tuesdays are supposed to be boring."

"Not anymore." Lana glances at the clock. "Isn't today when Fire Chief What's-His-Name was scheduled to do our annual inspection?"

The rolling pin freezes mid-roll. "No," I whisper. "That's next week."

The bell above the front door chimes. Through the kitchen window, I see Marjorie, my part-time cashier, straighten her spine and smooth her hair.

"Excuse me," says a voice I'd know anywhere, even after all this time. Deeper now, with a rasp that wasn't there before, but unmistakably his. "I'm looking for the owner."

Lana's eyes widen. She mouths, What do you want me to do?

I take a deep breath, untie my apron, and hang it on the hook. "I want you to keep making those pies," I say, surprised by how steady my voice sounds. "I'm going to go say hello to our new fire chief."

I walk through the swinging door, chin up, heart hammering. And there he is.

Jake Colton. Six feet of broad shoulders and faded jeans. The boyish face I remember is now weathered, more defined. A shadow of stubble along his jaw. Eyes still that impossible blue.

Those eyes find mine immediately. His confident smile falters.

"Annie," he says.

"Chief Colton," I reply, extending my hand like we're strangers. Like he didn't once know every secret I had. "Welcome back to Firelight Falls."

# *Jake*

I KNEW SEEING HER would knock the wind out of me. I just didn't expect it to hurt this much.

Annie Barrett stands before me, all five-foot-four of her looking ready for battle. Her hand extends professionally, but her green eyes are guarded. The freckles I once counted like stars are mostly faded now, but a few still dust her nose. Her brown hair is shorter than I remember, brushing her shoulders in soft waves.

"Thank you," I say, taking her hand. The touch is brief, businesslike, but it sends electricity up my arm, anyway. "It's good to be back."

The bakery smells like heaven—butter and sugar and something cinnamony in the oven. It's exactly what I pictured her future would look like. Warm. Inviting. Sweet with an edge, just like her.

"I heard you're here for the inspection," Annie says, retrieving a folder from beneath the counter. "Though you're early. We weren't expecting you until next week."

"Actually, I'm just here for coffee." I clear my throat. "And maybe to say hello."

She blinks, thrown off script. The teenagers behind me in line shuffle impatiently.

"Oh," she says. "Well, coffee I can do."

I follow her to the counter, acutely aware of the whispers around us, the stares boring into my back. Small towns never change. Neither, apparently, does my racing pulse whenever Annie's around.

"Black, two sugars?" she asks, and that she remembers feels like a victory I don't deserve.

"You remember," I say.

A flash of hurt, or maybe anger, crosses her face. "I remember everything, Jake."

The words land like a punch. I nod, accepting the hit because I've earned it. "I'm sorry," I say, though I know it's twenty years too late.

"For what?" She pours the coffee with steady hands. "For leaving? For not saying goodbye? Or for not calling even once in twenty years?"

Her voice stays professional, almost pleasant, but her eyes tell a different story. They always did. Annie could smile through anything, but her eyes always gave her away.

"For all of it," I say, my heart squeezing at the hurt behind her words.

She slides the coffee across the counter. "That'll be $3.50."

When I reach for my wallet, our fingers brush. She pulls back quickly, as if burned.

"I heard about your wife," she says, softer now. "I'm sorry for your loss."

"Thank you." The familiar ache spreads through my chest. Lisa's been gone three years, but grief has a way of sneaking up on you. "It's been an adjustment. For me and Maddie both."

"Your daughter?" Annie asks, and I nod. "How old is she?"

"Fifteen. All attitude and headphones." I smile. "She's a good kid, though. Just... struggling with the move."

Annie nods, and I see the questions in her eyes, the ones she's too polite to ask. Why here? Why now? Why her bakery on a Tuesday morning when I could've eased into this reunion?

"Dad?" A voice calls from the doorway, and I turn to see Maddie, hands shoved in her jacket pockets, dark hair falling across her face. "You said this would be quick. I'm going to be late."

"Sorry, honey." I gesture her over. "Come meet someone."

Maddie slouches to my side, all teenage reluctance. I see Annie's expression soften as she takes in my daughter's face. Maddie's beautiful, if I say so myself. She got Lisa's dark eyes, and my stubborn jawline.

"Maddie, this is Ms. Barrett. She owns this bakery."

"Annie," she corrects me, offering my daughter a genuine smile. "Nice to meet you, Maddie."

Maddie mumbles a hello, but her eyes linger on the pastry case. Annie notices and reaches for a chocolate croissant, sliding it into a bag.

"On the house," she says. "Welcome to Firelight Falls."

"Thanks," Maddie says, perking up slightly.

"We should go," I say, fishing out a five-dollar bill. "First day at the station. Wouldn't want to be late."

Annie nods, making change. When she places the coins in my palm, I hold her gaze.

"It really is good to see you, Annie."

She meets my eyes, and for a second, the mask slips. I see the girl I knew, the one who used to climb through my window when my dad was on a bender, the one who taught me how to dance for prom in her grandmother's kitchen.

"Take care, Jake," she says, and turns to the next customer.

As Maddie and I walk to my truck, my daughter looks at me sideways. "You know her," she says with a mouthful of croissant. "Like, really know her."

"Used to," I correct her, taking a sip of coffee that tastes exactly how I remember it should.

"Is she the reason we moved to this tiny town in the middle of nowhere?"

I start the engine, avoiding her too-perceptive gaze. "We moved here for Grandma," I say. "And because I got a good job offer."

Maddie snorts. "Right. And the way you looked at the baker lady had nothing to do with it."

I pull out onto Main Street, past the town square where Annie and I once carved our initials into a bench. Past the old movie theater where we had our first date. Past twenty years of memories I've never been able to outrun.

"Buckle up," I tell my daughter. "It's going to be an interesting ride."

# Annie

A WEEK PASSES BEFORE I see Jake again. Seven days of jumping every time the bakery door chimed , of rehearsing casual greetings in my bathroom mirror, of telling myself I'm over it.

Over him.

"He hasn't come back in," Lana points out as she helps me unload a delivery of flour. The early morning sun streams through the kitchen windows, painting everything gold. "Maybe he's avoiding you too."

"I'm not avoiding him," I lie, hefting a bag onto the metal prep table. "I'm busy. The Spring Bloom Festival is in three weeks, and Mayor Wilson wants me to coordinate the baking contest this year."

"Mmmhmm." Lana gives me that look, the one that says she sees right through me. "And that's why you sent Marjorie to deliver those pastries to the fire station yesterday?"

I brush flour from my hands. "Marjorie needs the delivery experience."

"Annie Barrett"—Lana plants her hands on her hips —"you've personally delivered to every business in this town for fifteen years. Try again."

"Fine." I reach for my apron, tying it with more force than necessary. "I'm giving him space. Is that so wrong? Twenty years of silence and suddenly he's here, with those eyes and that... that everything."

"That everything," Lana repeats with a smile. "Very specific."

"You know what I mean." I grab a whisk, needing something to do with my hands. "He broke my heart."

"When you were twenty-two," Lana reminds me gently. "People change."

"Some things don't." I crack eggs into a bowl, the familiar rhythm soothing my nerves. "He still takes his coffee black with two sugars. He still has that little scar by his eyebrow from when we were ten and he tried to rescue Mrs. Henderson's cat from a tree."

"And you still notice everything about him," Lana observes. "Look, I'm not saying forgive and forget. I'm just saying, maybe hear him out. Find out why he's really back."

"For his mother," I say automatically. "And the job."

Lana raises an eyebrow. "If you believe that, I've got some oceanfront property in West Texas to sell you."

Before I can respond, the bell above the front door chimes. Marjorie pokes her head into the kitchen, her eyes wide.

"Annie? The fire marshal is here for the inspection."

My heart skips, then races. "Scheduled?"

She nods. "On the calendar for today. Nine o'clock."

I glance at the clock: 8:55. I look down at my flour-covered apron, the streak of batter on my wrist. I haven't even brushed my hair since arriving at 5 AM.

"Tell him I'll be right out," I say, untying my apron.

Lana hands me a damp cloth. "You've got flour on your nose."

I wipe my face, smooth my hair, and take a deep breath. Professional. Polite. Distant. I can do this.

When I push through the swinging doors, Jake's standing by the counter in his official uniform. The navy blue brings out his eyes, and the badge on his chest catches the light. He looks authoritative, solid. The uniform suits him, I think, and then immediately scold myself for noticing.

"Good morning, Chief Colton," I say, keeping my tone professional. "You're right on time."

He looks up from his clipboard, and for a moment, I see surprise in his eyes. Maybe he was expecting Marjorie, too.

"Morning, Annie," he says, his voice warm. Then, more formally, "Ms. Barrett. I'm here for your annual inspection."

"Of course." I gesture to the bakery. "Where would you like to start?"

"Kitchen first, then storage areas, exits, fire extinguishers," he says, following me toward the swinging doors. "Should be pretty routine."

Nothing about this is routine, I think as we enter the kitchen. Lana gives us a bright smile and makes a flimsy excuse about needing to check inventory, leaving us alone among the mixers and cooling racks.

Jake moves through the space professionally, checking gauges on the ovens, inspecting the hood system over the stoves. His presence seems to fill every corner of my carefully organized domain. He makes notes on his clipboard, asks questions about capacity and procedures. I answer everything calmly, even as my pulse betrays me.

"Your fire extinguisher needs to be recertified," he says, examining the tag. "It expired last month."

"I'll take care of it today," I promise.

He nods, making a note. "Otherwise, everything looks good in here. Where's your storage room?"

I lead him to the back of the bakery, to the narrow hallway with supplies on one side and my small office on the other. The storage room is barely big enough for the two of us, lined with industrial shelving stacked with flour, sugar, and baking supplies.

"Watch your head," I warn as he ducks under a hanging rack of pans.

He steps carefully, his broad shoulders nearly brushing the shelves on either side. I'm suddenly, intensely aware of how small the space is, how close he stands.

"Your sprinkler system is up to code," he says, looking up at the ceiling. "When was the last time you had an electrician check these outlets?"

"Last spring," I say, inching backward to give him space. My heel catches on a bag of flour, and I stumble.

His hand shoots out, steadying me, warm against my elbow. The touch lasts only a second before we both pull away, but it's enough to send electricity racing up my arm.

"Sorry," I murmur.

"You're fine," he says, then clears his throat. "I mean, it's fine."

We make our way out of the storage room, and I exhale a breath I'd been holding. Jake checks the emergency exits, the circuit breaker, the evacuation routes. With each item on his list, I think we're almost done, almost through this painfully professional dance.

"Just one more thing," he says, flipping a page on his clipboard. "I need to check your upstairs apartment access and fire escape route."

I freeze. My apartment above the bakery is my sanctuary, my private space. The thought of Jake being there, seeing how I live, feels too intimate somehow.

"Is that really necessary?" I ask. "The access hasn't changed since last year's inspection."

"New chief, new inspection," he says with an apologetic smile. "I have to see everything myself. Regulations."

I nod stiffly and lead him to the back staircase. We climb in silence, my keys jingling nervously in my hand. At the top landing, I unlock the door and step inside, hyperaware of him following me.

My apartment is small but cozy. There's an open living room with a kitchen along one wall, and doors to a bedroom and bathroom off to the side. Morning light pours through the windows, drawing attention to the colorful throw pillows on my sofa, the bookshelf crammed with cookbooks, and the vase of fresh bluebonnets on my coffee table.

Jake stands in the doorway, taking it all in. I see my home through his eyes. I look around at the framed photographs on the wall (none of him), the handmade quilt from my grandmother draped over an armchair, the stack of romance novels on my coffee table.

"Nice place," he says.

"Thanks." I shift from foot to foot. "Fire escape is through the bedroom window. It was installed five years ago."

He nods and follows me into the bedroom. I'm suddenly grateful I made my bed this morning, that there aren't any clothes strewn about. The fire escape's a metal landing and staircase visible through the window.

Jake tests the window, making sure it opens easily. "Good clearance," he notes, writing something down. "No obstructions."

As he turns back to me, his eyes catch on something on my nightstand. I follow his gaze and my stomach drops.

The small wooden box that holds the pressed flower from prom, the movie ticket stubs, and the faded photographs I've never been able to throw away. The one with his initials carved into the lid... a gift for my sixteenth birthday.

He doesn't comment, but I see the recognition in his eyes, the slight softening of his expression.

"That should do it," he says, clicking his pen. "Everything looks good, Annie. You're up to code except for that fire extinguisher."

"I'll replace it today," I promise again, eager to get him out of my bedroom, out of my apartment, and away from the evidence that I never fully let him go.

We walk back downstairs in silence. At the bottom of the steps, he pauses.

"Annie," he says, his voice low. "I know this is awkward, me being back, doing these inspections... I just want you to know—"

"It's fine," I interrupt, not ready for whatever he's about to say. "You're doing your job. I respect that."

"It's more than that," he presses. "I..."

The kitchen door swings open, and Caroline Colton strides in, her sleek blonde hair pulled back in a perfect ponytail, her tailored blazer a stark contrast to my flour-dusted clothes.

"There you are," she says to Jake, then notices me. Her professional smile shifts to something warmer. "Annie Barrett. It's been a minute."

"Caroline," I say, genuinely happy to see her despite the timing. Jake's sister and I had been friends once, too, before her brother broke my heart and left town. "I heard you opened your law practice here."

"Divorce attorney," she confirms with a grim smile. "Turns out there's plenty of business even in a small town." Her eyes flick between Jake and me, taking in the tension. "Am I interrupting?"

"Just finishing an inspection," Jake says, holding up his clipboard.

Caroline's eyebrow raises slightly. "Well, when you're done playing Smokey Bear, we have that meeting with the mayor in twenty minutes."

Jake checks his watch and nods. "I'm done here." He turns to me, his expression professional once more. "You'll get your official paperwork by email, Ms. Barrett. Just take care of that extinguisher."

"I will. Thank you, Chief Colton."

He hesitates, like there's more he wants to say, but Caroline's already heading for the door. With a nod that feels wholly inadequate, he follows his sister.

I watch them go, Caroline's voice drifting back as the door closes: "So, how awkward was that on a scale from one to meeting-your-ex-at-your-high-school-reunion?"

The door clicks shut. I lean against the wall, exhaling slowly.

Just fire inspections and small talk for the next twenty years. I can handle that.

Can't I?

# Jake

"How awkward was that on a scale from one to meeting your ex at your high school reunion?" Caroline asks the moment we're outside.

"Not now, Care," I mutter, tucking my clipboard under my arm.

"That bad, huh?" My sister keeps pace beside me as we walk toward Town Hall. "You know, some might say it's a conflict of interest, inspecting your ex's business."

"It's my job," I say. "I inspect every business in Firelight Falls."

"Mmmhmm." Caroline's heels click purposely on the sidewalk. "And you just happened to schedule Annie Barrett's bakery as your first personal inspection."

I shoot her a look. "I'm being thorough."

"You're being obvious," she counters. "Mom told me you've been asking about Annie since you decided to move back. Real subtle, little brother."

"I was curious," I say, defending myself. "It's been twenty years."

"Twenty years, and you could have broken the silence at any point," Caroline reminds me. "A phone call. A Christmas card. A 'hey, sorry I vanished without a word after we'd been inseparable since kindergarten.'"

The guilt is familiar territory, worn smooth like river stones. "I know."

"Do you?" Caroline stops walking, forcing me to face her. "Jake, I love you. You're my brother. But what you did to Annie was cruel."

"I was trying to protect her," I say, the old excuse sounding hollow even to my own ears.

Caroline's expression softens slightly. "From what? Dad's drinking? Your rebellious phase? She knew all that, Jake. She loved you anyway."

I look away, down Main Street, where Firelight Falls is coming alive for the day. The hardware store owner is sweeping his sidewalk. The florist is arranging bouquets in her window display. This town, so familiar and yet changed in a thousand small ways during my absence.

"I was a mess back then," I say. "You remember what I was like after Dad's accident. The fights. The drinking. The motorcycle."

"I remember. I also remember Annie being the only one who could talk sense into you most days."

I close my eyes briefly, letting myself remember Annie climbing through my window after Dad had passed out drunk on the couch. Annie bandaging my knuckles after another fight. Annie holding me when I cried, the only person I'd let see that vulnerability.

"I didn't deserve her," I say finally. "I still don't."

Caroline sighs. "That wasn't your decision to make, Jake. It was hers."

We start walking again, the town hall coming into view. The Texas flag flutters beside the American one, both casting shadows on the stone steps.

"So, what's your plan now?" Caroline asks. "You're back. She's here. You're clearly still hung up on her."

"I'm not..." I begin, then stop at Caroline's skeptical look. "I don't have a plan. I'm here for Mom, and for Maddie. To give my daughter some stability."

"And running into Annie everywhere—at the grocery store, at church, at every town event—that's just a bonus?"

I don't answer, which is answer enough for my too-perceptive sister.

"Just be careful," Caroline says as we climb the town hall steps. "Annie's built a good life here. She's respected, successful. Don't blow back into town expecting to pick up where you left off."

"I'm not expecting anything," I say, but the wooden box on Annie's nightstand flashes in my mind. The one I carved for her all those years ago, apparently still treasured enough to keep close.

Inside the town hall, Mayor Wilson is waiting in the conference room, with a stack of papers on the table before him. He's in his sixties now, gray-haired but still robust, with the same booming voice I remember from childhood.

"Chief Colton! Ms. Colton! Right on time," he says, standing to shake our hands. "Have a seat. We've got the Spring Bloom Festival to discuss."

I take a seat across from Caroline, grateful for the distraction of work. The Spring Bloom Festival is one of Firelight Falls' biggest events of the year. Three days of carnival rides, contests, music, and food culminating in a massive lantern release that lights up the night sky over the town's signature waterfall.

"We'll need a comprehensive safety plan," Mayor Wilson is saying, sliding papers toward me. "Routes for emergency vehicles, staging areas, safety measures for the lantern release. The works."

I nod, scanning the preliminary plans. "I'll have a full assessment by next week."

"Excellent," the mayor says, then turns to Caroline. "And you, young lady, will be pleased to know you've been appointed to the organizing committee."

Caroline's professional smile doesn't waver, though I know she's mentally rearranging her caseload. "Happy to help, Mayor."

"You'll be working with Annie Barrett on the baking contest," he continues, and I feel Caroline's foot connect with my shin under the table. "She's heading it up this year."

"Is she?" Caroline says with exaggerated interest. "What a coincidence."

Mayor Wilson beams, oblivious to the subtext. "And Chief Colton, you'll be overseeing the lantern release and fireworks, naturally. You'll need to coordinate with the contest organizers on scheduling."

I keep my expression neutral. "Of course."

"The first planning meeting is tomorrow night, right here," the mayor continues. "Seven o'clock sharp. Full committee."

Which means Annie will be there. I'll have to sit across a table from her again, pretending we're nothing more than polite acquaintances.

The meeting continues, covering budgets and logistics and volunteer assignments. I take notes mechanically, my mind in a bakery storage room, with the scent of vanilla in the air and Annie's green eyes looking anywhere but at me.

When we finally leave city hall an hour later, Caroline hooks her arm through mine.

"Well, brother," she says with a smile that's half amusement, half concern. "Looks like the universe is determined to throw you two together."

"Or the mayor is," I mutter.

"Either way," Caroline says, "I'd suggest bringing your A-game to that committee meeting. And maybe some flowers."

"Flowers won't fix this," I say.

Caroline squeezes my arm. "No, but twenty years of groveling might be a start."

As we part ways at the corner, I glance back toward Annie's bakery. The scent of something sweet carries on the warm spring breeze, mixing with the fragrance of blooming bluebonnets lining the sidewalk.

Some fires, once started, never truly go out. They just wait, embers glowing, ready to ignite again at the slightest touch.

Tomorrow night, I'll see if ours still has any spark left at all.

# Annie

Spring in Firelight Falls means three things: bluebonnets painting the hillsides, tourists flooding Main Street to see our waterfall, and my specialty strawberry-rhubarb pies selling out before noon.

It also means, apparently, committee meetings.

I arrive at Town Hall ten minutes early, arms loaded with a box of pastries—my usual contribution for any gathering. The conference room is empty except for Mayor Wilson, who is arranging folders on the large oak table.

"Annie!" he booms, face lighting up at the sight of the bakery box. "You're a godsend. Coffee's brewing, but these will sweeten the deal."

I set the box on the refreshment table, unpacking an assortment of mini lemon tarts, blueberry muffins, and my newest creation, lavender shortbread with honey glaze.

"Trying to bribe the committee?" a voice asks from the doorway.

I turn to see Ben Martinez leaning against the frame, his police uniform crisp, his smile easy. Ben moved to Firelight Falls five years ago to become our town's deputy sheriff, and we've developed a comfortable friendship primarily based on his sweet tooth and my baking skills.

"Is it working?" I ask, sliding a muffin his way.

"Completely." He takes a bite, closing his eyes in appreciation. "I'm now prepared to vote your way on anything."

"Glad to hear it, Deputy." I laugh, arranging the remaining pastries. "Though I'm not sure what we're voting on yet."

"Festival budget, vendor placement, which teenager gets to be crowned Spring Bloom Queen." Ben ticks off on his fingers. "The usual."

More committee members filter in. The library director, the high school principal, and the owner of the hardware store. I'm arranging coffee cups when Caroline enters, looking polished in a floral blouse and pencil skirt despite the late hour.

"Tell me those are your lemon tarts," she says by way of greeting, making a beeline for the pastry box.

"Made fresh this afternoon," I confirm, handing her a napkin.

Caroline takes a delicate bite and sighs contentedly. "This is why I can never leave Firelight Falls. The city has fancy law firms, but they don't have Annie Barrett's tarts."

I'm about to respond when Jake walks in, and my carefully practiced casualness evaporates. He's changed out of his uniform into a simple blue button-down and jeans, but the badge clipped to his belt marks him as still on duty. Our eyes meet briefly before I look away, suddenly very interested in arranging and rearranging napkins.

"Evening, everyone," Jake says, nodding to the room at large.

The mayor claps his hands. "Excellent! We're all here. Let's get started."

We take our seats around the table. By some cosmic joke, or Caroline's strategic maneuvering, I end up directly across from Jake. I keep my eyes on Mayor Wilson as he launches into his spiel about the importance of the Spring Bloom Festival to our town's economy and community spirit.

"This year marks the festival's seventy-fifth anniversary," the mayor announces, "which means everything needs to be bigger and better than ever."

The meeting progresses through budget discussions and event scheduling. I take diligent notes, volunteering to coordinate with local farmers for the freshest produce for the baking contest. When it's Jake's turn to present safety measures for the lantern release, I allow myself to watch him.

He speaks confidently, outlining fire prevention protocols and emergency response plans. The others listen intently, nodding at his suggestions. This is Jake in his element. He's calm, in control, and responsible. So different from the wild, reckless boy I once knew.

"Chief Colton raises good points about the lantern release," Mayor Wilson says when Jake finishes. "Annie, since the baking contest finals will happen just before the lanterns, you two should coordinate on timing."

I nod stiffly. "Of course."

"Excellent!" The mayor beams. "Now, onto vendor placements."

The meeting drags on for another hour. When we finally adjourn, committee members linger over the remaining pastries, chatting about festival details. I gather my notes, eager to escape before I'm forced into a conversation with Jake.

Too late. As I reach for my purse, he appears at my side.

"Do you have a minute?" he asks quietly.

I consider saying no, claiming an early morning, but curiosity wins. "One minute."

He nods toward the door. "Outside?"

I follow him into the hallway, where the sounds of conversation fade. The town hall is quiet at this hour, the wooden floors gleaming under fluorescent lights. Jake stops near a bench beside a large window overlooking the town square.

"I wanted to talk to you about the inspection yesterday," he begins.

"If there's something else wrong with my kitchen..."

"No," he interrupts gently. "Everything's fine. Great, actually. I just... I felt like we left things awkward."

I cross my arms. "Things have been awkward for twenty years, Jake."

He winces slightly. "Fair enough."

"Is that all? Because I have an early start tomorrow."

"No, it's not." He takes a deep breath. "I owe you an explanation. For leaving. For... everything."

Part of me, a large part, wants to hear it. The other part is terrified of what he might say. "It was a long time ago."

"Not long enough to forget, apparently." His eyes are serious, searching mine. "Annie, I..."

The conference room door swings open, and committee members spill into the hallway. Ben approaches, holding my forgotten jacket.

"You left this," he says, glancing between Jake and me with barely disguised curiosity.

"Thanks," I say, relieved for the interruption. "I was just heading out."

"Me too," Ben says. "Walk you to your car?"

I nod, turning back to Jake. "We can talk about the festival coordination later. Good night, Chief Colton."

Something that looks suspiciously like jealousy flashes in Jake's eyes, but he nods. "Good night, Annie."

Ben and I walk out into the cool spring evening. Stars are just beginning to appear in the darkening sky, and the scent of wisteria hangs in the air.

"So," Ben says casually, "you and the new fire chief."

"Old friend," I say, keeping my tone light.

"Must have been some friendship," Ben observes. "Temperature dropped about ten degrees when he walked in."

I smile despite myself. "That obvious?"

"Only to everyone with functioning eyeballs." Ben bumps my shoulder gently. "Want to talk about it?"

"Not particularly."

"Fair enough." We reach my car, and he waits while I unlock it. "Just remember, I'm good at keeping secrets. And I'm a very patient listener."

"I'll keep that in mind. Thanks, Ben."

As I drive back to the bakery, my mind replays Jake's words. I owe you an explanation. Twenty years too late, a voice inside me insists. And yet, another voice whispers, Better late than never.

I park behind the bakery and climb the stairs to my apartment, too tired to even check the day's receipts. Tomorrow will be busy. Thursdays always are, and I need rest more than I need to dwell on Jake Colton and his explanations.

But sleep eludes me. I toss and turn, memories surfacing like bubbles in simmering water. Jake at seventeen, teaching me to drive in his beat-up Chevy. At twenty, dancing with me in my grandmother's kitchen. Jake at twenty-two, kissing me under the stars by the waterfall, promising forever.

Gone without a word the next day.

I give up on sleep around four and head downstairs to the bakery. Baking has always been my therapy. Today, I decide on cinnamon rolls. The recipe is complicated enough to demand my full attention.

The familiar routine soothes me. Mixing the dough, kneading it until it's smooth and elastic. Letting it rise while I prepare the filling of brown sugar, butter, cinnamon, and a hint of cardamom. Rolling the dough into a perfect rectangle, spreading the filling, and rolling it tight. The precision of slicing the log into even portions. The satisfaction of arranging them in pans, watching them rise again.

By the time Marjorie arrives at six, the bakery's filled with the scent of baking cinnamon rolls. I've also prepared two strawberry-rhubarb pies, a tray of croissants, and started the dough for the day's bread.

"Couldn't sleep?" Marjorie asks, hanging up her jacket.

"Spring allergies," I lie, pulling the rolls from the oven. Their tops are golden brown, the filling bubbling at the edges.

"Uh-huh." She eyes the abundance of baked goods. "Those allergy-induced cinnamon rolls smell amazing."

I smile and hand her an apron. "Help me frost these before we open?"

The morning rush keeps us busy. Locals stop in for coffee and breakfast on their way to work. Tourists ask for recommendations on the best spots to view the bluebonnets. The rhythm of transactions and conversations keeps me grounded.

At around ten, the bell chimes, and a dark-haired teenager slouches through the door. It takes me a moment to recognize Maddie Colton, Jake's daughter. She's alone, eyes scanning the pastry case with interest.

"Morning," I greet her. "What can I get you?"

She looks up, recognition dawning. "You're the baker lady. From before."

"Annie," I confirm. "And you're Maddie."

She nods, tucking a strand of hair behind her ear. The gesture is so like Jake's that my chest tightens.

"Is that chocolate croissant thing still available?" she asks, pointing to the case.

"Pain au chocolat," I say. "And yes, fresh this morning."

"I'll take one. And..." she hesitates, "a coffee? Black with sugar?"

Just like her father. I smile and prepare her order, wrapping the pastry in wax paper.

"Playing hooky?" I ask, nodding to her backpack.

"Study hall," she explains. "They let seniors go off campus if we have permission."

I hand her the coffee and pastry. "How are you liking Firelight Falls so far?"

She shrugs, the universal teenage gesture of noncommittal feeling. "It's okay. Small. Everyone knows everyone."

"That's both the charm and the curse," I agree.

"Dad says he grew up here," she says, studying me. "Did you know him? Back then?"

The question catches me off guard. "Yes," I say cautiously. "We were friends."

"Just friends?" She raises an eyebrow in a way that's distinctly Caroline-like. Apparently, the Colton women share that particular talent.

I feel my cheeks warm. "It was a long time ago."

Maddie takes a sip of her coffee, wincing slightly at the bitterness. "Dad doesn't talk much about before. About my mom, sure, but not about growing up here."

I'm not sure how to respond to that. What has Jake told his daughter about his past? About us?

Before I can think of a reply, the back door bangs open. Lana bursts in, her apron smeared with something red.

"Annie, we've got a problem," she says breathlessly. "The stove—"

As if on cue, the fire alarm blares to life, its shrill sound cutting through the bakery. Smoke seeps through the kitchen door.

"Everyone out!" I call, already moving toward the kitchen. "Marjorie, make sure all customers exit safely."

"Annie, don't—" Lana starts, but I push past her into the kitchen.

Smoke billows from the industrial stove where a pot of strawberry compote has boiled over, flames licking up from the burner. I grab the fire extinguisher from the wall, yank the pin, and aim at the base of the fire.

The extinguisher sputters, then stops.

The expired extinguisher. The one I promised Jake I'd replace.

The flames grow higher, catching the paper towels nearby. Smoke thickens, stinging my eyes and throat. I back away, searching for something else to smother the flames.

"Annie!" Jake's voice cuts through the chaos. He appears beside me in full turnout gear, oxygen mask pushed up on his head. "Out. Now."

"My kitchen..."

"Now." His tone brooks no argument. He guides me firmly toward the exit while two other firefighters tackle the blaze.

Outside, a small crowd has gathered. Marjorie is talking to customers, ensuring everyone got out. Maddie stands on the sidewalk, her coffee and pastry forgotten, eyes wide. When she spots Jake, her shoulders visibly relax.

"Is everyone accounted for?" Jake asks Marjorie, who nods.

"What happened?" I ask Lana, who's dabbing at her apron.

"The strawberry compote," she explains. "I turned away for one minute to answer the phone. It boiled over, caught fire. I tried to smother it, but..."

"It's okay," I assure her, though my heart races at the thought of what could have happened. I could've lost my grandmother's recipes, her antique rolling pins, the bakery itself, my home and livelihood.

Jake approaches after conferring with his team. He's removed his helmet, and sweat dampens his hair. "Fire's out," he says. "Damage is minimal. Mostly smoke, and some scorching around the stove."

Relief floods me. "Thank you."

His expression hardens. "You promised you'd replace that extinguisher."

"I know, I—"

"You could have been hurt," he cuts in, voice tight. "Or worse. What were you thinking, running toward a fire?"

"It's my bakery," I say defensively. "My responsibility."

"Your responsibility is to evacuate safely and let professionals handle it," he counters. "This isn't a debate, Annie. You know better."

I bristle at his tone. "Don't lecture me, Jake. I've been running this bakery for fifteen years without incident."

"And today could have changed that in seconds." His eyes flash with fear. "If we hadn't been just down the street on another call..."

"But you were," I point out. "And everything's fine."

Jake runs a hand through his hair. "This time," he says, quieter now. "This time everything's fine."

One of the other firefighters calls to him, and he turns away. "We'll need to file a report," he says over his shoulder. "And inspect the kitchen before you reopen."

"Fine," I say stiffly.

As he walks back to his team, Maddie approaches me. "Are you okay?" she asks.

"I'm fine," I assure her. "Just a little smoke inhalation. I'm sorry about your breakfast."

She waves it off. "Does Dad always yell at fire victims?"

Despite everything, I laugh. "I'm not exactly a victim. And no, I think that was special treatment."

She studies me thoughtfully. "He was really scared. I could tell."

Before I can respond, Jake returns. "Maddie, you should get back to school."

"I have study hall," she reminds him.

"Not anymore," he says firmly. "Officer Martinez is waiting to drive you back."

Maddie rolls her eyes but obeys, giving me a small wave as she leaves. Jake turns to me.

"We're clearing the building now," he says, all professional again. "There's some damage to your stove hood and the wall behind it. You'll need to have it repaired before you can use it again."

The reality sinks in. The bakery will need to close, at least for a few days. During tourist season. Right before the Spring Bloom Festival.

"How long?" I ask.

"Couple of days, maybe a week, depending on how fast repairs can be made." His expression softens slightly. "I'm sorry, Annie. I know this is your busiest season."

I nod, throat tight. "What do I do now?"

"Wait for the all-clear, then you can go back in to assess." He hesitates. "You have insurance?"

"Of course," I say, though I'm already dreading the paperwork.

Jake looks like he wants to say more, but another firefighter calls him over to sign something. With a nod, he leaves me standing on the sidewalk, watching smoke dissipate from my bakery windows.

Lana squeezes my shoulder. "It'll be okay," she says. "We'll figure it out."

I nod, trying to believe her. Behind us, I hear Jake issuing orders, his voice steady and sure. The same voice that just scolded me like a child, that almost offered explanations the night before, that once whispered promises under starlight.

The irony isn't lost on me. A fire brought Jake Colton back into the heart of my life, just when I thought I could keep him safely at its edges.

# Jake

"THIRD-DEGREE BURNS," CAROLINE SAYS, settling into the chair across from my desk. "That's what Annie would give you if she heard you were still brooding."

I look up from the incident report I've been staring at for the past hour. "I'm not brooding. I'm completing paperwork."

"On a kitchen fire that was out in under five minutes?" Caroline picks up the framed photo of Maddie on my desk, studies it, and sets it down. "Must be fascinating reading."

I sigh and push the report aside. I've been replaying this morning's scene in my mind. I can't get the image of Annie standing there with a useless extinguisher out of my mind. I keep thinking of what could've happened if we hadn't been nearby.

"She could've been hurt," I say.

"But she wasn't," Caroline points out. "And yelling at her in front of half the town probably didn't help your reconciliation efforts."

"I wasn't trying to reconcile. I was doing my job."

Caroline gives me her lawyer look. The one that says she sees right through me. "Is that why Maddie texted me that you 'went full fire chief' on Annie?"

"Maddie should have been in school," I mutter.

"Jake." Caroline leans forward. "This is the second time in twenty-four hours you've had a chance to talk to Annie like a normal human being, and instead, you've hidden behind your badge."

"I'm not hiding," I protest. "I'm trying to keep this town safe. Including Annie."

"Especially Annie," Caroline corrects. "Look, I get it. Seeing her in danger pushed your buttons. But if you want any chance of fixing things between you, you might try an approach that doesn't involve clipboards and safety lectures."

I rub my eyes, suddenly tired. "Who says I'm trying to fix things?"

"Please." Caroline leans back. "You've been carrying a torch for that woman longer than some marriages last. That's why you're really back in Firelight Falls."

"I'm back for Mom," I remind her. "And to give Maddie stability."

"And it's just a coincidence that your high school sweetheart lives here?" Caroline shakes her head. "You forget I've known you your entire life, little brother. I can read you like a fire safety pamphlet."

I crack a smile despite myself. "Shouldn't you be terrorizing opposing counsel somewhere?"

"Later. Right now, I'm handling a more challenging case. Your love life." She stands, smoothing her skirt. "Call Annie. Apologize for being a jerk. Offer to help with the repairs."

"The insurance will cover repairs."

"Not what I meant, and you know it." She heads for the door. "Or don't call her. Keep brooding. But remember, you're not the only single man in Firelight Falls, and the deputy seemed awfully concerned about walking her to her car last night."

After Caroline leaves, I try to focus on paperwork, but my mind keeps drifting to Annie in her smoke-filled kitchen. To the bakery, her pride and joy, now temporarily closed. To Ben Martinez and his easy smile.

I pick up my phone, then set it down again. What would I even say? Sorry I yelled at you for nearly burning down your business. Want to grab coffee at the only other cafe in town?

Before I can overthink it further, my office door opens again. Chief Williams, my second-in-command and a thirty-year veteran of the Firelight Falls Fire Department, pokes his head in.

"Got a minute, Chief?"

I gesture to the chair Caroline just vacated. "What's up, Bill?"

Chief Williams settles his substantial frame into the chair. "Just got off the phone with Mayor Wilson. He's concerned about the bakery closing right before tourist season."

"We all are," I say. "But safety regulations..."

"I know, I know." Williams waves a hand. "But he had an idea. The community center kitchen's commercial grade, up to code, and only used for the senior lunch program three days a week."

I see where this is going. "You want to offer it to Annie?"

"Mayor's already cleared it with the town council. She could use it to fulfill existing orders, maybe even handle limited retail with a table set up out front." Williams shrugs. "Just until her place is repaired."

It's a good solution. A small olive branch after this morning's confrontation. But it also means more interaction with Annie, more chances for me to stick my foot in my mouth.

"I'll pass along the information," I say carefully.

Williams studies me. "Heard you two have a history."

Small towns. Nothing stays private for long. "Ancient history."

"Didn't sound too ancient this morning, from what I heard." Williams stands. "Just a piece of advice from an old firefighter... sometimes the hardest blazes to put out are the ones that have been smoldering for years."

After he leaves, I sit for a long moment, turning over his words. Then, I reach for my keys and head for the door. Some messages are better delivered in person.

I find Annie at the bakery, standing on the sidewalk with a building inspector. Her hair's pulled back in a messy ponytail, and smudges of soot still mark her cheeks. She looks exhausted but determined as she takes notes on a clipboard.

I hang back until the inspector leaves, then approach cautiously. She notices me and straightens, her expression guarded.

"Come to issue more citations, Chief Colton?" she asks.

I deserve that. "Actually, I came with a proposition. From the mayor."

Interest flickers in her eyes. "What kind of proposition?"

"The community center kitchen," I explain. "It's available for you to use until your repairs are complete. Commercial grade, already up to code."

Surprise registers on her face, followed by cautious hope. "Really? That would help a lot."

"I can show you the space now, if you have time," I offer.

She hesitates, glancing back at her bakery. "I should wait for the insurance adjuster."

"They won't be here until tomorrow," I say. "I checked."

Annie studies me as if trying to determine my motives. Finally, she nods. "Okay. Let me grab my purse."

We walk to my department SUV in awkward silence. As we drive the short distance to the community center, I search for something to say that won't sound like another lecture.

"How bad's the damage?" I ask finally.

"Mostly the stove and hood, some of the wall and ceiling," she says, looking out the window. "The insurance should cover it, but the inspector says it'll take at least a week for repairs."

"I'm sorry," I say, and mean it. "I know how important the bakery is to you."

She glances at me, surprise softening her features. "Thank you."

We arrive at the community center, a brick building near the town park. The kitchen's in the back. Annie walks through it slowly, opening cabinets, checking appliances, mentally calculating how she can adapt her workflow.

"It could work," she admits. "The oven capacity is actually better than mine."

"Less charm, though," I observe, taking in the stark white walls and fluorescent lighting.

Annie smiles faintly. "I can bring some of that with me."

We stand there in the sterile kitchen, the silence between us less strained now. Annie runs her hand along a stainless steel counter, lost in thought.

"I'm sorry about this morning," I say. "For yelling. It wasn't professional."

She looks up, those green eyes assessing me. "No, it wasn't."

"I saw the smoke, knew it was your place, and just..." I trail off, not sure how to explain the fear that had gripped me.

"Reverted to fire chief mode?" she suggests.

"Something like that."

Annie sighs, leaning against the counter. "I should've replaced the extinguisher. You were right about that."

"Still..."

"No, let me finish." She straightens. "I've spent fifteen years building that bakery. Everything I have is tied up in it. When I saw the fire, I just reacted. It wasn't smart, but it was instinct."

I understand that better than she knows. The need to protect what matters, regardless of risk. It's what drove me to become a firefighter after my reckless youth. What drove me away from her all those years ago.

"I get it," I say simply.

She studies me, a hint of her old warmth in her gaze. "Do you? Because the Jake Colton I remember wasn't exactly known for careful risk assessment."

I smile despite myself. "People change."

"So I've heard." She pushes off the counter. "This kitchen will work. Thank the mayor for me."

"You can thank him yourself at the committee meeting tomorrow night," I remind her.

Annie groans. "I'd forgotten about that. I guess the universe really wants us working together."

"Seems that way." I hesitate, then decide to take a risk. "Maybe after the meeting, we could grab coffee? Have that talk that keeps getting interrupted?"

Surprise flickers across her face, followed by wariness. "Jake..."

"Just coffee," I clarify. "And answers to whatever questions you have about why I left. Why I came back. You deserve that much."

Annie considers this for a long moment. Outside, spring rain pats against the windows, soft and steady.

"Okay," she says finally. "Coffee. After the meeting."

Relief washes through me. It's a small step, but a step nonetheless. "I'll drive you back to the bakery."

As we walk to the SUV, the rain picks up, turning the world misty and silver. Annie tilts her face up to the sky, letting the drops fall on her cheeks, washing away the last traces of soot.

"Remember when we got caught in that downpour junior year?" she asks suddenly. "After the spring concert?"

The memory of us running through rain much heavier than this, seeking shelter under the gazebo in the town square, both of us soaked to the skin and laughing surfaces immediately.

"You wore that green dress," I say, the details suddenly vivid. "Your mom was furious about the mud stains."

Annie looks surprised I remember. "You gave me your jacket to wear home."

"It looked better on you, anyway."

A ghost of a smile touches her lips, and for a moment, we're just Annie and Jake again, sharing memories untainted by what came after.

Then thunder rumbles in the distance, breaking the spell. We hurry to the SUV as the rain intensifies.

"Some things never change," Annie says as we pull away from the curb. "Spring storms in Firelight Falls."

Other things do change, I think.

People.

Circumstances.

Chances.

One thing remains constant, though... the feeling in my chest whenever she's nearby, warm and steady as a flame.

# Annie

THE COMMUNITY CENTER KITCHEN has excellent appliances but terrible acoustics. Every clang of a mixing bowl and every thud of a rolling pin echoes off the institutional white walls. By noon, my head's pounding.

"More coffee?" Lana asks, already pouring a cup from the industrial-sized coffee maker.

"Please." I accept the mug gratefully. "This place is efficient but exhausting."

It's been three days since the fire, and we've established a rhythm of sorts. Mornings are for bread and basic pastries, which we sell from a makeshift counter in the community center lobby. Afternoons are dedicated to special orders and preparations for the Spring Bloom Festival, now just over two weeks away.

"At least the ovens are reliable," Lana says, gesturing to the perfect rows of cupcakes cooling on racks. "And we haven't lost very many customers."

She's right. Our regulars have been loyal, following us to this temporary location. Some have even brought small touches to make the sterile space feel more like a bakery. They've dropped off potted plants, a vase of fresh-cut bluebonnets, hand-drawn signs from the elementary school children, and other little things to make us feel more at home.

"The insurance adjuster called," I tell her, checking my phone. "Repairs should be finished by next Friday."

"Just in time for the festival," Lana notes. "Speaking of which, isn't that committee meeting tonight?"

I nod, focusing intently on the buttercream I'm mixing. The meeting. The coffee after. This is the conversation I've been both dreading and anticipating for twenty years.

"You're going, right?" Lana presses.

"I have to. I'm coordinating the baking contest."

"That's not what I meant, and you know it." She lowers her voice, even though we're alone in the kitchen. "Are you really going to have coffee with him afterward?"

"It's just coffee," I say, echoing Jake's words from the other day. "And answers."

"Finally," Lana mutters. She's heard the story of Jake's disappearance countless times over our decade of friendship. "Are you nervous?"

I consider lying, but what's the point? "Terrified," I admit. "What if his reason for leaving is something I can't forgive? What if it's something I can?"

Lana squeezes my shoulder. "Either way, you'll know. And knowledge is power, right?"

"Knowledge is complicated," I counter, but I smile at her attempt to cheer me up.

The afternoon passes in a blur of buttercream and fondant as we prepare for a large wedding order. By closing time, I'm covered in a fine dust of confectioner's sugar, and my feet are aching.

"Go home," Lana urges. "Shower. Change. Mentally prepare for whatever bombshell Jake's going to drop."

"You're not helping," I groan, but I take her advice, heading back to my apartment above the bakery.

The insurance company has assured me that the living space is safe, even while repairs continue downstairs. Still, the lingering smell of smoke greets me as I climb the stairs. I throw open the windows, letting in the fresh spring air, then head for the shower.

Under the hot spray, I try to organize my thoughts. What do I actually want from this conversation with Jake? Closure? Understanding? Something more? Twenty years is a long time to hold onto anger, to wonder what might have been. But seeing him again has reopened wounds I thought had already healed.

By the time I've dressed in clean jeans and a soft green blouse that brings out my eyes, I've settled on a simple goal—to just listen. Whatever Jake has to say, I'll hear him out. Then decide what it means for now, for us, if there even is an 'us' to consider.

The committee meeting's already underway when I arrive at Town Hall, slipping into an empty seat with a murmured apology for my tardiness. Jake sits across the table, and our eyes meet briefly before I look away, focusing on Mayor Wilson's updates about the lantern vendors.

As the meeting progresses, I present my plans for the baking contest, explaining the categories, judging criteria, and timeline. Jake follows with revised safety protocols for the lantern release, his voice steady. We're both the picture of professional cooperation, giving no hint of the tension simmering beneath the surface.

"One more item before we adjourn," Mayor Wilson announces, beaming at us all. "The Spring Queen coronation. Traditionally, our fire

chief and the contest coordinator lead the opening dance at the Spring
Bloom Ball. Chief Colton, Ms. Barrett, I trust you're both agreeable?"

My head snaps up. Dance? With Jake? In front of the entire town?

"Actually, Mayor," I begin, searching for a graceful way to decline.

"We'd be honored," Jake cuts in smoothly. All eyes turn to me awaiting
my confirmation.

I force a smile. "Of course."

"Excellent!" Mayor Wilson claps his hands. "That concludes our
business for tonight. Next meeting, same time next week."

As the room empties, Jake approaches my chair. "Ready for that
coffee?"

I nod, gathering my notes. "As I'll ever be."

He holds the door for me. "The Bluebonnet Cafe?"

"Too many ears," I say, thinking of the town's gossip network. "The
waterfall park might be better."

Jake nods. "I'll drive."

We ride in silence to the small park that overlooks Firelight Falls,
the town's namesake. At this time of year, the waterfall is at its most
impressive, fed by spring rains. Even at night, with just the park's ambient
lighting, the cascade of water shimmers against dark rocks.

Jake produces a thermos of coffee from his truck, along with two
stainless steel cups. "I came prepared," he explains, pouring the steaming
liquid.

We settle on a bench overlooking the falls, the rush of water
providing both soothing white noise and a convenient barrier against
eavesdroppers.

"So," I say, wrapping my hands around the warm cup. "You wanted to
talk."

Jake takes a deep breath. "I owe you an explanation."

"Yes. You do."

He stares out at the waterfall for a long moment, gathering his thoughts. "Do you remember the night before I left? We were here. Not this exact spot, but down by the water."

I remember. A warm May night, stars reflected in the pool below the falls. With Jake's arms around me, his promises whispered against my hair. "I remember."

"I meant everything I said that night," he whispers, "about loving you. About wanting a future together."

"Yet you were gone the next day," I say, unable to keep the edge from my voice. "No note. No call. Just gone."

Jake nods, accepting the accusation. "My dad called that night after I dropped you home. He was drunk, but lucid enough to tell me he'd gotten into trouble again. Serious trouble."

Tommy Colton's drinking had been a constant shadow over Jake's teenage years. By the time we were seniors, his father had progressed to harder stuff, spiraling deeper after Jake's mother left him.

"What kind of trouble?" I ask.

"Gambling debts. To people you don't want to owe money to." Jake's jaw tightens at the memory. "He'd dug himself into a hole so deep there was no climbing out. They were threatening him and threatening to come after Caroline."

"So you left to protect her," I surmise. "To protect your family."

"Yes." Jake turns to look at me, his eyes reflecting the park lights. "Dad had a cousin in Houston who said he could get me work on an offshore rig. Good money, fast. I knew I could earn enough to pay off the debts if I went right away."

"But why not tell me? Why just disappear?"

He runs a hand through his hair, a gesture so familiar it makes my chest ache. "Because I knew you'd insist on coming with me, or waiting for me. And I couldn't ask that of you, Annie. You had college plans, dreams. Your grandmother needed you here."

"That wasn't your decision to make," I say, the old hurt rising.

"I know that now," he acknowledges. "I was twenty-two, scared, trying to protect everyone I loved. I thought I was doing the right thing by setting you free, not tying you to my family's mess."

"So you went to Houston," I prompt, needing to hear the rest.

"For a while. Then offshore, like my dad's cousin promised. The work was hard and dangerous, but it paid well. Within a year, I'd made enough to clear Dad's debts." Jake's voice grows quieter. "By then, I had heard you were doing well in college. Dating someone new."

My mind flashes to Michael, the business major I'd dated briefly my sophomore year. A relationship born more of loneliness than connection, it had fizzled after a few months.

"Caroline told you that," I guess.

Jake nods. "She thought it would help me move on. And maybe I needed to believe it."

"So you stayed away."

"I enrolled in the fire academy in Houston," he continues. "Found I had a knack for helping people in crisis. It gave me purpose, a way to channel all that reckless energy into something good."

"And then?" I prompt, knowing there's more to the story. Worth twenty more years.

"I met Lisa during a fire safety event at her elementary school. She was a teacher, kind, patient." A small smile touches his lips at the memory. "We got married when Maddie was on the way. Built a life in Houston. It was good, Annie. Not what I'd planned at twenty-two, but good."

I swallow around the lump in my throat. It shouldn't hurt to hear that he'd been happy with someone else, but it does. "I'm glad," I say, and mostly mean it.

"After Lisa got sick," Jake continues, his voice rougher now, "things changed. Cancer's not a fast fight. Three years of treatments, remissions, setbacks. When she passed, Maddie and I were both lost."

"I'm sorry. Truly."

"Mom's health started declining around the same time," he says. "Her hip, her heart. Caroline was handling everything alone. When the fire chief position opened up here, it felt like... I don't know. A sign, maybe."

"So you came back," I say. "For your mother and for Maddie."

Jake meets my eyes directly. "For them, yes. And to make things right with you, if I could."

The confession hangs between us, as tangible as the mist from the waterfall. I take a sip of coffee, buying time to process everything he's said.

"That's a lot to take in," I say finally.

"I know." Jake sets his cup down. "I don't expect forgiveness, Annie. I just wanted you to know the truth. I never stopped caring about you. Never stopped wondering what might've been."

Such simple words for such a complicated feeling. I've wondered the same thing in quiet moments over the years. What if he'd stayed? What if I'd gone with him? What if, what if, what if?

"Thank you for telling me," I say, surprising myself with how steady my voice sounds.

"Does it help?" he asks. "Knowing?"

"I'm not sure yet," I admit. "Twenty years is a long time to wonder. It's going to take more than one conversation to process."

Jake nods. "I understand."

We sit in silence for a while, watching the waterfall, each lost in our own thoughts. Finally, I gather the courage to ask a question that's been nagging at me.

"Why agree to the dance at the Spring Ball?"

Jake turns to me, his expression softening. "Because some things I've missed more than others. Dancing with you in your grandmother's kitchen. Making you laugh. Being part of your life, even in a small way... Those are the things I've missed the most."

His honesty catches me off guard. I expected evasion, maybe a casual brush-off. Not this directness.

"I don't know what happens next," I tell him truthfully. "I'm not the same person I was at twenty-two. Neither are you."

"No," he agrees. "But maybe that's okay. Maybe we get to find out who we are now, to each other."

It's a dangerous suggestion, full of potential for both healing and fresh heartbreak. Part of me wants to run from it, to protect the life I've carefully built without him. Another part, the part that kept his wooden box on my nightstand for twenty years, wants to leap at the chance.

"One step at a time," I say finally. "Starting with not embarrassing ourselves at this dance."

Jake smiles, relief clear in his eyes. "Does that mean you'll practice with me? I'm rusty."

"We'll see," I say, but I'm fighting a smile of my own. "I should get home. I have an early start tomorrow."

We walk back to his truck, the night air cool against my skin. As we drive through the sleeping town, I realize something has shifted between us. Not forgiveness, exactly, but understanding. A foundation perhaps, for whatever comes next.

Jake pulls up to the town hall, where my car's parked. "Thank you for listening," he says.

"Thank you for explaining," I reply. "Good night, Jake."

As I climb the stairs to my apartment later that night, I realize I feel lighter somehow. The weight of questions I've carried for twenty years has lifted. In its place is a feeling of possibility, and sleep comes easier than I expected.

# Jake

"So? How'd it go?" Caroline ambushes me in my kitchen the next morning, having let herself in with the spare key I now regret giving her. "Did you grovel appropriately? Did she forgive you? Are you getting married next week?"

"Good morning to you, too," I say, pouring a second cup of coffee. "And slow down. It was one conversation."

"A twenty-year-overdue conversation." She accepts the coffee I offer her. "Details, please."

I lean against the counter, considering how much to share. "I told her everything. About Dad's debts, the job offshore, why I left."

"And?"

"And she listened. Said she needed time to process."

Caroline studies me over the rim of her mug. "That's actually better than I expected. I half thought she'd throw the coffee in your face."

"The thought may have crossed her mind," I admit. "But Annie's never been the type for dramatic gestures."

"Unlike some Coltons I could name," Caroline says pointedly. "So what happens now?"

I tell her about the Spring Ball dance tradition since she missed the planning meeting. Caroline's eyebrows shoot up.

"The mayor's playing matchmaker," she declares. "Classic small-town meddling."

"Or he's just following tradition," I counter, though I had the same suspicion.

"Please." Caroline waves this away. "Half the committee are charter members of the Firelight Falls Gossip Brigade. They're all watching you two like it's their personal soap opera."

She's probably right, which means everyone in town will scrutinize our dance. No pressure.

"I invited her to practice," I say. "She didn't exactly say yes."

"But she didn't say no. That's progress."

After Caroline leaves for work, I head to the station, my mind only half on the day's duties. Chief Williams notices my distraction during the morning briefing.

"Everything alright, Chief?" he asks as the other firefighters file out.

"Just thinking about the Spring Bloom Festival," I say, which isn't entirely a lie.

"Big responsibility," he agrees. "First major event under your watch. But you've got a good team here."

I nod, grateful for the vote of confidence. In the month since taking over as chief, I've grown to appreciate the close-knit nature of the Firelight Falls Fire Department. These men and women know the town's quirks well.

"Any word on how Miss Barrett's bakery repairs are coming along?" Williams asks a little too casually.

I suppress a smile. The gossip network is clearly operational. "Insurance adjuster says they should be finished by the end of next week."

"Good, good." Williams nods. "She's a fine woman, Annie Barrett. Backbone of this community."

"So I've noticed," I say neutrally.

"Makes the best peach cobbler this side of the Mississippi, too." He gives me a knowing look. "Just an observation."

Before I can respond, the alarm sounds. A brush fire on the edge of town, likely sparked by a discarded cigarette. We mobilize quickly, and I'm grateful for the distraction.

The fire's contained within an hour, more smoke than actual danger. By mid-afternoon, I'm back at the station, completing paperwork, when the front desk calls up.

"Chief, you've got a visitor."

I head downstairs, surprised to find Annie in the lobby, a large bakery box in her arms.

"Hi," she says, looking almost as surprised to see me as I am to see her. "I was just dropping these off. A 'thank you,' for the community center kitchen."

I lift the lid to find an assortment of pastries, including cinnamon rolls, blueberry muffins, and what look like peach hand pies. "The department will demolish these in about ten minutes flat," I predict.

"That's the idea." She shifts uncomfortably. "How was your day?"

"Small brush fire, nothing serious. Yours?"

"Three wedding cake consultations and a birthday order for twins." She smiles. "The community center kitchen is working out well."

I'm about to respond when the station's overhead speakers crackle to life. "Attention all personnel. Tomorrow's training drill will now include a simulated mass casualty event. All shifts report at 0800."

Annie raises an eyebrow. "Sounds intense."

"Standard procedure," I explain. "We run these scenarios monthly to stay sharp."

A thoughtful expression crosses her face. "Would you need volunteers? For the casualties?"

I blink, surprised by the offer. "You want to volunteer?"

"Why not?" She shrugs. "The community center kitchen is closed on Thursdays. Lana and I could help. Might be interesting to see what you actually do all day."

The idea of Annie taking part in our drill is both appealing and nerve-wracking. "It can get pretty realistic," I warn. "Fake blood, simulated injuries."

"I've watched enough medical dramas to handle it," she says with a confidence I'm not sure is warranted. "Besides, I'm curious."

I consider the logistics. We'd been planning to use off-duty firefighters and police as victims, but having civilian volunteers would actually make the scenario more realistic.

"If you're serious, we could use the help," I admit. "Eight AM, here at the station. Wear something you don't mind getting messy."

"Perfect." She turns to go, then pauses. "Oh, and about the dance practice... my grandmother's old record player still works. Friday evening, seven o'clock sound good? I'll make dinner."

She's gone before I can respond, leaving me standing in the lobby with a box of pastries and a stunned expression.

Chief Williams appears beside me, eyeing the bakery box. "Progress?" he asks.

I can't help but smile. "Maybe."

• • • • ● • ● • • • •

The next morning dawns clear and mild, perfect weather for an outdoor training exercise. By seven-thirty, the station is buzzing with activity as firefighters prepare equipment and review protocols. At precisely eight, Annie arrives with Lana in tow.

"Reporting for casualty duty," she announces with a mock salute.

I introduce them to our training coordinator, who ushers them away to be briefed and made up with realistic-looking injuries. The scenario we've planned simulates a building collapse at the old textile factory on the edge of town. It's a complex rescue operation requiring coordination between multiple teams.

When I next see Annie, she's lying on the ground outside the mock disaster site, her arm positioned at an unnatural angle and her face artfully streaked with fake blood and dust. Lana is nearby, pinned under a carefully constructed "debris" piece that looks alarmingly real.

"Ready?" I ask, crouching beside Annie.

"Ready," she confirms. "Though I think they went a little overboard with my makeup."

"That's the idea," I say, fighting a smile. "Just follow the paramedics' instructions when they reach you."

The drill begins with a simulated dispatch call. My teams deploy systematically, assessing the scene, establishing command posts, and beginning triage of victims. I oversee operations from the command center, periodically throwing in new challenges like a secondary collapse, a gas leak, or a missing victim.

From my position, I can see Annie being assessed by one of our paramedics. She's playing her role convincingly, answering questions about her "injuries" and allowing herself to be moved onto a backboard. There's something surreal about watching my team treat the woman I once thought I'd spend my life with, even in this simulated context.

The drill lasts nearly three hours, with multiple phases of rescue, treatment, and transport. By the end, everyone's exhausted but satisfied with the execution. Our civilian volunteers, including Annie and Lana, gather in the station's conference room for debriefing and refreshments.

"That was intense," Lana declares, wiping fake blood from her forehead. "But kind of amazing to watch you all work."

Annie nods in agreement. "I had no idea there was so much coordination involved. So many moving parts."

"That's the point of these exercises," I explain. "To practice until every step becomes second nature."

"Well, I'm impressed," Annie says, and her genuine admiration warms me more than I care to admit.

After the debrief, as volunteers and firefighters disperse, Annie lingers. She's cleaned most of the fake blood and dirt from her face, though traces of it still stain her t-shirt.

"Thank you for letting us take part," she says. "It was eye-opening."

"Thank you for volunteering," I reply. "It made the scenario more realistic."

She studies me for a moment. "This is really your calling, isn't it? Emergency management, keeping people safe."

I nod. "It gives purpose to all the chaos I used to carry around. Channels it into something useful."

"I get that," she says. "It's how I feel about baking. Taking separate ingredients, some that wouldn't be pleasant on their own, and creating something people love."

The parallel strikes me as unexpectedly profound. We've both found ways to transform our natural tendencies into careers that serve others.

"Still on for tomorrow night?" I ask. "Dance practice?"

"Seven o'clock," she confirms. "I remember how you take your steak."

As she turns to leave, I'm struck by the strangeness of this new dynamic between us. We're not quite friends, definitely not strangers, but suspended in some undefined middle space with the weight of shared history and unspoken possibilities.

"Annie," I call after her. She turns back, eyebrow raised. "Thank you for giving me a chance to explain."

She nods, a small smile playing on her lips. "See you tomorrow, Chief Colton."

The title sounds different somehow when she says it. Almost like she's teasing me. Like we're sharing a private joke about my official role versus the boy she once knew.

As I watch her walk away, still bearing traces of our simulated disaster, I'm reminded of something my training officer once told me. Sometimes, the most important part of rescue work isn't the technical skills or equipment. It's recognizing when someone's ready to be saved.

I just can't decide which of us is the rescuer, and which is the one in need of saving.

# Annie

"You're having him over to your apartment?" Lana's voice rises in disbelief as she helps me knead bread dough in the community center kitchen. "For dinner? And dancing?"

"It's just practice," I insist, trying to downplay the flutter of nerves I've been feeling all day. "For the Spring Bloom Ball. It's tradition."

"Uh-huh." Lana gives me a knowing look. "And the home-cooked meal? The music? The mood lighting I bet you're planning?"

I feel my cheeks warm. "I'm not planning mood lighting."

"But you're not denying the rest," she points out, triumphant. "Annie Barrett, you're falling for him again."

"I am not," I protest, perhaps too quickly. "I'm just... processing. Getting to know who he is now."

After our coffee talk by the waterfall, and learning why Jake left all those years ago, something has shifted between us. A willingness to move forward instead of remaining locked in the past.

"Processing," Lana repeats skeptically. "With steak and dancing."

I roll my eyes. "It's not a big deal."

"If it's not a big deal, why did you ask me to finish the Henderson wedding cake so you could leave early to prepare?" She gestures to the elaborate three-tier cake we've been working on all morning.

"Because I haven't cooked a proper meal in my apartment since the fire," I explain. "I need to air it out, make sure everything's working properly."

It's a flimsy excuse, and we both know it. I've spent far too much time thinking about this dinner. About seeing Jake in my space, not as the fire chief conducting an inspection, but as... whatever we are to each other now.

"Just be careful," Lana says, her teasing tone giving way to genuine concern. "I don't want to see you hurt again."

"I know," I assure her. "I'm going in with eyes wide open."

But as I leave the community center early that afternoon, my thoughts drift back to closed eyes and racing hearts, to a time when Jake Colton was the center of my world.

* * * * * * * * * *

*Seventeen Years Old - Spring in Firelight Falls*

"Annie! Over here!"

Jake's voice carries across the crowded school parking lot, where students are gathering for the annual Spring Carnival fundraiser. He stands by his beat-up Chevy, waving enthusiastically, unself-conscious in a way most teenage boys aren't.

I wave back, weaving through clusters of classmates to reach him. His smile widens as I approach, his impossibly blue eyes bright with excitement.

"I signed us up for the three-legged race," he announces proudly.

"You did what?" I stare at him in disbelief. "Jake, I'm the clumsiest person in Firelight Falls. I trip over flat surfaces."

"Exactly why you need a strong partner." He flexes dramatically, making me laugh despite my reservations. "Come on, Annie. It'll be fun."

Fun. Jake's favorite word. His life philosophy, really. While I calculate risks and plan ahead, Jake dives into experiences headfirst, pulling me along in his wake. It's been this way since we were kids, since he moved in next door and decided we would be best friends.

"Fine," I relent, as we both knew I would. "But when we end up face-down in the mud, I reserve the right to say I told you so."

"Deal." He grins, slinging an arm around my shoulders as we walk toward the carnival. The casual touch sends warmth spreading through me, a new and increasingly familiar sensation whenever Jake is near.

Things have been changing between us lately. Lingering looks. Excuses to touch. Conversations that stretch late into the night, deeper than our usual banter. Neither of us has acknowledged it aloud, this subtle transformation from childhood friendship to... something else.

The carnival is in full swing when we arrive, the school football field transformed with booths, games, and food stands. Streamers flutter in the spring breeze, and the air smells of popcorn and cotton candy.

"Let's get something to eat before the race," Jake suggests, already steering us toward the food trucks.

We share a basket of fries and wander through the carnival, trying our luck at various games. Jake wins a small stuffed bear at the ring toss and presents it to me with exaggerated formality.

"For you, m'lady," he announces with a bow.

I curtsy in return, playing along. "Why, thank you, kind sir."

Our eyes meet, and for a moment, the carnival noise fades away.

The moment breaks when Caroline appears, clipboard in hand, her blonde ponytail swinging. At nineteen, Jake's sister is home from college for the weekend, volunteering as the carnival coordinator.

"There you are," she says to Jake. "The three-legged race starts in ten minutes. Get to the starting line."

Jake salutes her dramatically. "Yes, ma'am."

Caroline rolls her eyes, then gives me a knowing look. "Good luck, Annie. You'll need it with this one as your partner."

At the starting line, volunteers tie our inside legs together with a colorful bandana. Jake's leg is warm against mine, our hips pressed together out of necessity.

"Strategy," he says, suddenly serious. "We need to match our rhythms. Inside arms around each other, outside arms for balance."

I nod, trying to focus on his instructions rather than our proximity. "Countdown, then start with the inside foot."

"See?" Jake grins. "We're already in sync."

The starting whistle blows, and we're off. Our first few steps are wobbly, but we quickly find our rhythm.

"Inside, outside, inside, outside," Jake chants, his arm firm around my waist.

We're actually doing well, pulling ahead of the pack, when a rock or divot, I'll never know which, catches our joined feet. I feel the stumble begin, the inevitable fall approaching in slow motion.

Jake's arm tightens around me as we go down, somehow twisting so that he takes the brunt of the impact. We land in a tangled heap on the grass, laughing too hard to care about the race continuing without us.

"You okay?" he asks, still holding me close.

"I told you so," I reply, making him laugh harder.

We lay there for a moment, catching our breath, still tied together. Jake's face is inches from mine, his laughter fading into something softer, more intense.

"Annie," he says, his voice different somehow.

My heart pounds as he leans closer. Is this it? After years of friendship, are we finally going to cross that line?

"Time to untie the losers!" Caroline announces, appearing above us with scissors in hand, shattering the moment.

Jake helps me up after we're separated, his hand lingering in mine. "Raincheck?" he asks quietly.

I'm not sure if he means the race or... the other thing. But I nod anyway.

Later that evening, as the carnival winds down and twilight settles over Firelight Falls, we find ourselves at the waterfall viewpoint, watching the last rays of sun turn the cascade to liquid gold.

"Sorry about the race," Jake says, leaning against the railing beside me.

"Are you kidding? That was the most fun I've had in ages." It's true. Everything with Jake is fun, even falling on my face in front of half the school.

He turns to look at me, his expression suddenly serious. "Can I ask you something?"

My pulse quickens. "Of course."

"Do you ever think about... us? About how we're different lately?"

The directness of the question takes my breath away. Jake has always been brave in a physical sense. But this is a different kind of courage.

"Yes," I admit, matching his honesty with my own. "I think about it a lot."

Relief flashes across his face. "Me too. All the time, actually."

We stand there, balanced on the edge of something momentous. The waterfall roars below us, constant and changing all at once, like the feelings swirling between us.

"Annie," Jake says, taking a step closer. "I think I'm falling in love with you. I think maybe I have been for a long time."

The words hang in the air between us, beautiful and terrifying. This is Jake. My best friend, the one person who knows all my secrets and loves me, anyway. If we take this step, everything changes.

"I'm scared," I whisper, honest in a way I can only be with him. "What if we ruin everything?"

"What if we don't?" he counters. "What if it's amazing?"

That's Jake. Always seeing the possibility, the adventure, the upside.

"I think I'm falling in love with you too," I confess, the words both frightening and freeing.

The smile appearing on his face can light up the entire town. Slowly, giving me time to pull away if I wanted to, Jake leans in. Our first kiss is gentle, questioning, a little awkward as first kisses tend to be. But then something clicks into place, and suddenly it's as natural as breathing.

When we finally break apart, Jake rests his forehead against mine. "Worth the wait," he murmurs.

As stars appear above us, Jake takes my hand, our fingers interlacing with practiced ease. A gesture unchanged from our childhood, yet now charged with new meaning.

"You're my best friend, Annie Barrett," he says. "That doesn't change. We're just adding to it."

In that moment, I believe him completely. We are Jake and Annie, best friends since forever, now something more. And nothing—nothing—could ever pull us apart.

· · · · ● · ● · ● · · ·

The memory fades as I unlock my apartment door, arms laden with groceries for tonight's dinner. That day at the carnival had been the beginning. The start of five years as best friends who were also each other's first love. Five years of shared secrets, quiet promises, and plans for forever.

Until the day Jake disappeared, taking all those promises with him.

I set the groceries on the counter and open the windows, letting in the fresh spring air. The repairs to the bakery below are progressing well. The smell of smoke has faded, replaced by the scent of fresh paint and sawdust.

As I prep the steaks for marinating—salt, pepper, a touch of garlic, just how Jake likes them—I can't help wondering if I'm making a mistake. Opening this door to the past, to the man who walked away once before.

He had his reasons, a voice inside me argues. Good ones.

Protecting his family from his father's gambling debts, sparing me from being tied to his troubles... I understand his motivations now. But understanding doesn't automatically heal twenty years of hurt, wondering, or what-ifs.

By six-thirty, the apartment is ready. Steaks marinating, potatoes prepped for roasting, green beans cleaned and waiting. I've changed into a casual green dress. It's nothing fancy, just a step up from my usual jeans and t-shirt. My grandmother's record player sits in the corner, a stack of vinyl beside it.

At precisely seven o'clock, a knock sounds at my door. I take a deep breath, smooth my dress, and open it.

Jake stands there in dark jeans and a light blue button-down that brings out his eyes. His hair is still damp from a shower, and he's holding a bouquet of spring wildflowers.

"Hi," he says, a hint of nervousness in his smile. "These are for you."

"Thank you." I accept the flowers, their sweet scent filling the space between us. "Come in."

Jake steps inside, looking around with interest. Though he's been here before for the fire inspection, this feels more intimate, more deliberate.

"Smells amazing," he says, following me to the kitchen. "Steak?"

"Medium-rare, if you still take it that way," I confirm, arranging the flowers in a vase.

"Some things never change." His smile is warm, appreciative. "Can I help with anything?"

I set him to work on the salad while I get the potatoes into the oven. We move around each other in the small kitchen with surprising ease, falling into a rhythm that feels both new and familiar.

"How's the community center kitchen working out?" Jake asks as he slices cucumbers.

"Better than expected," I admit. "Less charming than the bakery, but the equipment is top-notch. And the locals have been incredibly supportive."

"This town loves you," Jake observes. "I've heard nothing but praise since I've been back. I've been told all about your cinnamon rolls and wedding cakes. Your contribution to every fundraiser and community event."

I feel my cheeks warm. "I just do what I can. Like my grandmother taught me."

"How is Martha?" Jake asks. "I've been meaning to visit her at Sunset Pines."

"She has good days and bad," I say, a familiar sadness creeping in. "The dementia's progressing. Some days she knows me. Some days she thinks I'm my mother."

Jake's hand touches my shoulder briefly. "I'm sorry. She was always so good to me."

"She asks about you on her lucid days," I admit. "Wants to know if that 'nice Colton boy' ever came back to town."

A shadow crosses Jake's face. "I should have come back sooner. Should have visited her, and you, and everyone."

"You're here now," I say softly, surprised by how much I mean it.

Our eyes meet, and for a moment, I'm seventeen again, standing by the waterfall with my heart in my throat, everything possible.

The timer beeps, breaking the spell.

"Potatoes," I murmur, turning away to check the oven.

We finish preparing dinner in comfortable silence, occasionally brushing against each other in the small space. By the time we sit down at my small table, the initial awkwardness has faded into something more relaxed.

Jake takes a bite of steak and closes his eyes in appreciation. "Perfect," he declares. "I'm surprised you remembered."

"Hard to forget your very specific steak preferences," I tease. "Especially after that disastrous cookout at the lake when my dad tried to serve you well-done."

Jake laughs, the sound warming me more than I care to admit. "That poor man. I thought he was going to disown me on the spot."

"He got over it," I assure him. "Eventually."

The conversation flows easily through dinner, touching on safe topics—Jake's work at the fire station, my plans for expanding the bakery's wedding business, Maddie's adjustment to Firelight Falls High School.

"She's settling in," Jake says, pride evident in his voice. "Even joined the yearbook committee. And she can't stop talking about your chocolate croissants."

"She's welcome anytime," I tell him. "She reminds me of you, actually. That same directness."

"God help me." Jake groans. "One of me was trouble enough."

As we clear the dinner plates, Jake notices the record player in the corner. "Is that still your grandmother's old Victrola?"

"The very same," I confirm. "Still works perfectly."

"May I?" he asks, already moving toward the collection of vinyl.

I nod, watching as he browses through the records, his fingers moving reverently over the worn album covers. He selects a Nat King Cole record and carefully places it on the turntable.

The first notes of "Unforgettable" fill the apartment, rich and warm. Jake turns to me, extending his hand.

"Practice makes perfect," he says with a small smile.

I hesitate only briefly before stepping into his arms. One hand finds my waist, the other clasps mine gently. My free hand rests on his shoulder, feeling the solid strength beneath his shirt.

We move, a little stiffly at first, finding our footing. It's been years since I danced with anyone, longer still since I danced with Jake. But muscle memory is a powerful thing, and soon we're swaying in perfect sync.

"Not bad," I observe as he guides me in a gentle turn. "You haven't forgotten everything."

"Some things stay with you," he whispers, his eyes holding mine. "No matter how much time passes."

My heart quickens as we continue to move together, the space between us gradually diminishing with each measure of music.

"Do you remember teaching me to dance?" Jake asks. "For senior prom?"

"In my grandmother's kitchen," I recall. "You were convinced you had two left feet."

"I was terrified of embarrassing you," he admits. "The baseball star who couldn't figure out a simple box step."

"You learned quickly," I remind him, following as he leads me into that very pattern.

"I had an excellent teacher." His hand presses slightly firmer against my waist, drawing me closer. "And motivation."

The song changes to "When I Fall in Love," and our steps slow to match the tempo. We're barely moving now, just swaying together, my head almost resting on his shoulder.

"I missed this," Jake murmurs, his breath warm against my hair. "Dancing with you."

I should pull away. Maintain distance. Protect myself from the possibility of being hurt again. But I lean into him, giving in to the comfort of his embrace.

"I missed it too," I confess.

The admission hangs between us, honest and vulnerable. Jake's hand releases mine, both arms encircling my waist now. My hands link behind his neck, and we're not so much dancing as holding each other while the music plays on.

"Annie," he says softly, pulling back just enough to meet my eyes. "I know it's complicated between us. I know twenty years is a long time. But being here with you, like this... it feels right."

My heart races, torn between past and present, caution and desire. "Jake—"

A sharp knock at the door interrupts whatever I might have said. We step apart quickly, like teenagers caught by parents.

"Expecting someone?" Jake asks, his voice slightly rough.

I shake my head, moving to answer the door. When I open it, I find Ben Martinez standing in the hallway, still in his police uniform.

"Ben," I say, surprised. "Is everything okay?"

"Sorry to bother you so late," he says, then notices Jake over my shoulder. "Oh. I didn't realize you had company."

An awkward silence falls as Ben takes in the scene. The record player is still spinning, the remains of dinner for two laid out on the table, and Jake standing in the middle of my living room looking decidedly domestic.

"What can I help you with?" I ask, trying to dispel the tension.

Ben seems to collect himself. "Just following up on the bakery break-in report. We caught the kids who smashed your window last week. Teenagers, like we suspected."

"That's good news," I say, though I'd almost forgotten about the minor vandalism incident in the wake of everything else. "Thank you for letting me know."

"No problem." Ben shifts uncomfortably. "I should let you get back to your evening. Sorry for the intrusion."

"It's fine," I assure him. "Thank you for stopping by."

After Ben leaves, I close the door and turn back to Jake, finding him with an unreadable expression.

"Everything okay?" he asks.

"Fine," I say. "Just some kids who broke a window at the bakery last week. Nothing serious."

Jake nods, but something has shifted in the room. The intimate moment from before has dissipated, replaced by an uncertain tension.

"It's getting late," he says finally. "I should probably go. Early shift tomorrow."

Part of me wants to ask him to stay, to pick up where we left off. But perhaps the interruption was for the best. A reminder to move slowly, to think clearly.

"Of course," I say. "Thank you for coming."

At the door, Jake pauses. "Tonight was nice, Annie. Really nice."

"It was," I agree, meaning it.

He hesitates, then leans in slowly, a question in his eyes. When I don't step away, he presses a soft kiss to my cheek, his lips lingering just a moment longer than necessary.

"Good night," he murmurs, pulling back reluctantly.

"Good night, Jake," I reply, my voice steadier than I feel.

After he leaves, I return to the living room and switch off the record player. The sudden silence is almost deafening. I should be cleaning up, washing dishes, preparing for tomorrow's early start at the community center kitchen.

Instead, I find myself at the window, watching Jake walk to his truck parked below. Just before he gets in, he looks up as if sensing my gaze, and raises a hand in farewell.

I wave back, my cheek still warm from his kiss, my mind full of memories both old and new.

Old flames, it seems, are the hardest to extinguish. And perhaps, the most dangerous to rekindle.

# Jake

THE DRIVE HOME FROM Annie's apartment is a blur, my mind replaying every moment of the evening. How comfortable we were cooking together, sharing memories over dinner. The way she felt in my arms as we danced, her body gradually relaxing against mine.

And then Martinez showing up, looking at Annie with undisguised interest.

I grip the steering wheel tighter, forcing myself to relax. I have no claim on Annie, no right to feel the jealousy that had surged through me at the deputy's appearance. Twenty years is a long time. Of course, there have been other men in her life. Just as there was a Lisa in mine.

My throat tightens at the thought of my late wife. What would she think of all this? Lisa had known about Annie, about my first love and how it ended. In the early days of our marriage, during late-night conversations, I'd confessed the entire story of my abrupt departure, my cowardice in not saying goodbye, and the regret I'd carried.

"You should write to her," Lisa had suggested once. "Explain what happened."

But I hadn't. Too much time had passed, and I'd convinced myself Annie was better off without the complications I would bring into her life. And then Maddie came along, and my focus shifted entirely to our growing family.

Now, pulling into my driveway, I wonder if things might have been different if I'd taken Lisa's advice. If I'd reached out years ago instead of letting the silence between Annie and me stretch into decades.

The house is dark when I enter, except for a small lamp in the living room. Maddie's at Caroline's for the night, having negotiated a sleepover with her aunt to work on a school project. The silence feels oppressive after the warmth of Annie's apartment.

I drop my keys on the counter and notice a missed text from Caroline.

> Caroline: How's the dance lesson going? Details tomorrow, or I'll make your life miserable. Love you!

I smile despite myself. Some things never change. My sister's nosiness chief among them.

Upstairs, I change and get ready for bed, but sleep seems unlikely. I'm too wired, too full of conflicting emotions. I pull a small wooden box from the back of my closet.

Inside are the few mementos I've kept. Ticket stubs from our first movie date, a dried flower from prom, photos yellowed with age. And letters, dozens of them, written over the years but never sent. Letters explaining, apologizing, wondering about her life. A record of my regret, preserved in ink and paper.

I select one at random, unfolding the creased page. The date at the top reads 2010. The year Maddie started kindergarten.

*Annie,*

*Maddie lost her first tooth today. She was so proud, bouncing around the house, showing everyone who came by. It made me think of us that summer when you lost three teeth in two weeks and worried you'd look like a jack-o'-lantern forever. Remember how I pulled your last baby tooth when you were too scared to wiggle it? You were so brave, closing your eyes and squeezing my hand while I counted to three...*

I fold the letter back, chest tight with memories. Every milestone in my life without Annie has been shadowed by moments of wondering what she would think. What would she say? Would she be proud of the man I've become?

Now I have the chance to find out. The realization both excites and terrifies me.

My phone buzzes with a text, pulling me from reflection.

> Annie: Thank you for tonight. The dance committee will be impressed.

I smile at the deliberate lightness of her message.

> The pleasure was all mine. Though I think we need a few more practices before we're ready for public viewing.

Her response comes quickly.

> Annie: Is that your subtle way of asking for another dinner invitation?

> Is it working?

Three dots appear as she types, disappear, then appear again.

> Annie: Maybe.

> Annie: Goodnight, Jake.

Goodnight, Annie. Sweet dreams.

I set the phone down, knowing sleep will be long in coming tonight. Tomorrow brings a full day at the station, final preparations for the Spring Bloom Festival, and an evening visit to see my mother at Sunset Pines.

But for now, I allow myself to linger in the memory of Annie in my arms, her head nestled against my shoulder as we swayed to music that had followed us through the years.

For the first time since returning to Firelight Falls, I let myself believe that maybe, we can find our way back to each other after all.

# Annie

THE BAKERY LOOKS ALMOST new. Fresh paint gleams on the walls, the hood over the stove shines with industrial polish, and the faint scent of sawdust lingers in the air. After a week of repairs, we're finally back home.

"What do you think?" I ask Lana, who's surveying the renovated space with a critical eye.

"I think I'm going to miss that fancy convection oven at the community center," she admits. "But this is home."

I nod, running my hand along the freshly sealed countertop. "We reopen tomorrow. Grand 'we survived a kitchen fire' celebration."

"Complete with commemorative flame-shaped cookies?" Lana suggests with a grin.

"Too soon," I protest, though I'm smiling too.

The bell above the front door chimes, and Marjorie pokes her head into the kitchen. "The fire marshal's here for the final inspection," she announces.

My heart does a little flip-flop, which I studiously ignore. "Send him back."

Lana gives me a knowing look before discreetly disappearing into the storage room, leaving me alone when Jake enters. He's in full uniform today, clipboard in hand, looking every inch the professional fire chief.

"Chief Colton," I greet him, aiming for businesslike despite the memory of dancing in his arms just days ago.

"Ms. Barrett," he replies, with warmth in his eyes. "Ready for inspection?"

I gesture to the renovated kitchen. "As we'll ever be."

Jake moves through the space methodically, checking fire extinguishers (all new and properly certified), smoke detectors, electrical work, and ventilation systems. I follow a few steps behind, watching as he makes notes on his clipboard.

"Everything looks good," he says finally. "The contractors did quality work."

"I made sure of it," I assure him. "I was here every day, checking in."

"Of course, you were." His smile is fond, knowing. "You've never been one to leave important things to chance."

"Unlike some people I know," I say, then immediately regret it when his expression flickers.

"I deserved that," he acknowledges quietly.

An awkward silence falls between us. We haven't seen each other since our dinner three nights ago, both busy with festival preparations and work commitments. The easy connection we'd found while dancing seems suddenly distant, overshadowed by the weight of our complicated history.

"I didn't mean—" I begin.

"It's okay," he interrupts. "Really. I know there's a lot we still need to talk about."

I nod, grateful for his understanding. "How are the festival security plans coming along?"

He accepts the change of subject gracefully. "Nearly completed. The committee approved the emergency response protocols yesterday. We're as ready as we can be."

"Good," I say. "Because the baking contest entries close today, and we're already at capacity. Twenty-five contestants in four categories."

"Sounds like you've got your hands full too." He signs something on his clipboard and tears off a copy, handing it to me. "This is your official clearance. You're approved to reopen."

"Thank you," I say, accepting the paper. Our fingers brush in the exchange, sending a familiar tingle up my arm.

Jake clears his throat. "So, tomorrow's the big reopening?"

"Yes, the doors open at six."

"I might stop by," he says casually. "For a congratulatory pastry."

The thought of seeing him in the morning sends a flutter through my stomach that I refuse to acknowledge. "There will be plenty," I assure him.

He nods and turns to leave. At the door, he pauses. "Annie?"

"Yes?"

"I'm glad you're back in your space. I know how much it means to you."

The simple observation, the recognition of what the bakery represents in my life, touches me deeply. "Thank you, Jake."

After he leaves, Lana reappears, eyebrows raised expectantly. "Well?"

"We passed inspection," I say, waving the clearance form.

"And?"

"And nothing." I move to the sink, busying myself with washing utensils. "He might stop by tomorrow for the reopening."

"Mmm-hmm."

"It's not like that," I insist.

"Then why are you blushing?" she counters.

Before I come up with a suitable response, my phone rings. The screen shows a number I don't recognize.

"Annie Barrett," I answer.

"Ms. Barrett? This is Mandy from Sunset Pines. I'm calling about your grandmother."

My heart drops. "Is she okay?"

"She's fine," Mandy assures me quickly. "But she's having one of her confused days, and she's asking for someone named Paul? Says she needs to tell him something important. We thought maybe calling you might help calm her down."

Relief mingles with concern. "I'll be right there."

After explaining the situation to Lana, I grab my purse and keys. The drive to Sunset Pines takes just ten minutes, one of the blessings of small-town living. The assisted living facility is a pleasant, one-story building surrounded by gardens just beginning to bloom with spring flowers.

At the reception desk, I sign in and am directed to the community room, where I find my grandmother sitting by a window, looking out at the garden. At eighty-eight, Martha Barrett remains elegant even in confusion, her silver hair neatly styled, her posture straight.

"Grandma?" I say softly, approaching her chair. "It's Annie."

She turns, her eyes, the same green as mine, clouded with confusion. "Annie, dear. Have you seen Paul? I need to talk to him about the dance."

My chest tightens. In her mind, she's back in time, when she would dance in the kitchen with Grandpa.

"Paul's not here right now," I say gently, taking the seat beside her. "But I can tell him whatever message you have."

She frowns, distressed. "But the festival is this Saturday. We need to practice."

I take her hand, wrinkled and spotted with age but still strong. "I'll make sure he practices, Grandma. I promise."

This seems to satisfy her. "You're a good girl, Annie. Jake loves you, you know. I can see it in his eyes."

My heart aches. If only love had been enough for him to talk to me instead of running away. "I know, Grandma," I say, because it's easier than explaining the complicated reality.

"Don't let him get away," she continues, patting my hand. "Some loves only come once in a lifetime."

I swallow hard against the lump forming in my throat. "I'll remember that."

We sit together for a while longer, her mind drifting between past and present. Eventually, she grows tired, and a nurse helps her back to her room for a nap.

As I prepare to leave, Mandy approaches me. "She has asked for Paul several times this week," she informs me. "Is there any chance he could visit? Sometimes seeing the actual person can help orient them."

I shake my head. "Paul was my grandfather. He passed away a long time ago," I say.

Mandy pats my shoulder. "I'm sorry," she says before heading down the hallway to help someone else.

On the drive back to the bakery, my mind churns. Hearing my grandmother talk about Jake, about love that comes once in a lifetime, has stirred up emotions I've been trying to keep contained.

Back at the bakery, I throw myself into reopening preparations, focusing on the comforting rhythm of mixing, kneading, and baking. By closing time, the display cases are stocked for tomorrow, and the kitchen is spotless.

As Lana and I lock up, a familiar truck pulls into the parking space behind the building. Jake steps out in jeans and a faded t-shirt.

"Hey," he calls, approaching us. "How did everything go with your grandmother?"

I blink in surprise. "How did you know about that?"

"Small town," he reminds me with a slight smile.

"Oh."

"Is she okay?" he asks, genuine concern in his voice.

"Just confused. Asking for Grandpa. I think she misses dancing in the kitchen."

A soft smile touches his lips. "I remember those kitchen dances, and later on the lessons she gave me. She was an excellent dancer."

Lana, who has been silently observing our exchange, clears her throat. "Well, I should get going. Jamie has a soccer game tonight." She gives me a meaningful look. "Don't stay too late, Annie. Early start tomorrow."

After she leaves, Jake and I stand in the bakery parking lot, the setting sun casting long shadows around us.

"Want to show me the renovations?" he asks, nodding toward the bakery. "Officially, I've seen everything, but I'd like the owner's tour."

"Sure," I agree, unlocking the back door again.

Inside, I lead him through the bakery, pointing out the improvements, including the new shelving in the storeroom, and the expanded prep area.

"They did good work," Jake observes as we complete the circuit back to the kitchen.

"They'd better have, considering what it cost," I say ruefully. "Even with insurance covering most of it."

Jake leans against the counter, studying me. "You've built something special here, Annie. I hope you know that."

"I do," I say, a hint of pride creeping into my voice. "It wasn't easy, especially in the beginning. Convincing the bank to loan money to a twenty-four-year-old with more enthusiasm than business experience."

"I'm not surprised you convinced them. You've always been persuasive when you believe in something."

The compliment warms me, but also stirs up questions I've been avoiding. "Is that why you didn't say goodbye? Because you knew I'd talk you out of leaving?"

The abrupt shift catches him off guard. He straightens, his expression growing serious. "Partly," he admits. "But mostly because I knew saying goodbye to you would be the hardest thing I'd ever done, and I wasn't sure I'd be strong enough to leave if I had to look you in the eye."

His honesty disarms me. "And now? Coming back, seeing me again... is it what you expected?"

Jake takes a step closer, his eyes never leaving mine. "Nothing about seeing you again has been what I expected, Annie. It's been... more."

"More what?" I press, my heart racing.

"More everything," he says simply. "Being around you again, it's like coming home and discovering it's both—exactly as I remembered and completely different at the same time."

The description captures exactly how I've felt since his return. "I know what you mean."

We stand there, the air between us charged with unspoken feelings. Jake's eyes drop briefly to my lips, and for a moment, I think he might close the distance between us.

Instead, he takes a deliberate step back. "I should let you get home. Big day tomorrow."

The moment breaks, and I nod, both relieved and disappointed. "Right. The reopening."

"I'll be there," he promises. "Save me a cinnamon roll?"

"I'll set one aside," I agree, following him to the door.

Outside, the spring evening has turned cool, the stars just beginning to emerge in the deepening blue sky. Jake pauses by his truck, keys in hand.

"Annie," he says, his voice serious again. "I know we still have a lot to work through. Things I need to explain better, questions you need to ask. But I want you to know, I'm not going anywhere this time. Not unless you ask me to."

The quiet promise settles around my shoulders like a warm hug. "Good night, Jake," I say.

"Good night, Annie."

I watch his truck disappear down the street before heading to my apartment upstairs, my mind full of emotions. The practical part of me warns against trusting too quickly, against opening my heart to the possibility of being hurt again. But the part that kept his wooden box on my nightstand for twenty years whispers some chances are worth taking, even when they come with risk.

As I prepare for bed, I remember my grandmother's words. Some loves only come once in a lifetime.

I fall asleep wondering if that's true, and if Jake Colton is my once in a lifetime love.

# Jake

THE MORNING OF ANNIE'S bakery reopening dawns clear and mild, perfect spring weather. I arrive just after six, joining the line of customers already forming outside the front door. The "Grand Reopening" banner flutters in the gentle breeze, and through the windows, I can see Annie and her staff bustling about, putting final touches on display cases.

At precisely six-thirty, she unlocks the door to cheers and applause from the waiting crowd. Her smile is radiant as she welcomes everyone inside, her cheeks flushed with excitement and a hint of nervous energy.

I hang back, letting others go ahead of me, content to watch Annie in her element. She moves through the bakery with practiced ease, greeting regulars by name, answering questions about the renovation, ringing up sales with efficiency that never feels rushed.

When I finally reach the counter, her smile softens. "Chief Colton. Right on time."

"Wouldn't miss it," I say, glancing at the nearly depleted pastry case. "Looks like a success already."

"Beyond expectations," she agrees. "Your cinnamon roll is safe, though." She reaches beneath the counter and produces a paper bag, slightly warm to the touch. "As promised."

"Thank you." Our fingers brush as I accept the bag, a now-familiar spark passing between us. "How long are you working today?"

"Until closing," she says. "I want to be here for the full day, make sure everything runs smoothly."

I nod, understanding her need to oversee this important reopening personally. "Maybe I could stop by afterward? We could grab dinner somewhere?"

She hesitates. "I'm not sure what time I'll finish. There's inventory to take, and the day's receipts to reconcile..."

"No pressure," I assure her quickly. "Another time."

She studies me for a moment, then seems to decide. "Actually, why don't you come by around eight? I should be done by then, and we could order takeout and eat upstairs."

Warmth spreads through my chest at the invitation. "I'd like that."

The line behind me grows restless, and Annie gives an apologetic smile. "Duty calls."

"Go save the hungry masses," I tell her. "I'll see you tonight."

The rest of my day is filled with final festival security preparations, a minor traffic accident on Main Street, and a planning meeting with county emergency services. By late afternoon, I'm back at the station, completing paperwork, when my phone buzzes with a text from Caroline.

Mom's having a rough day. Can you stop by Sunset Pines after your shift?

I reply immediately, Of course. Is everything okay?

She's agitated. Keeps asking about Dad.

My heart sinks. Our father has been gone for five years, and they were separated for over twenty, but on her bad days, Mom still asks for him. I'll head over now, I text back.

At Sunset Pines, I find Caroline sitting beside our mother's bed, holding her hand and speaking softly. Mom looks smaller than I remember, frailer somehow, though it's only been a few days since my last visit.

"Jake's here, Mom," Caroline says as I enter. "See?"

Mom looks up, her eyes unfocused. "Tommy?" she asks, using Dad's name.

"No, Mom," I say gently, taking her other hand. "It's Jake. Your son."

She frowns, studying my face. "Jake is just a boy. You're a man."

"I grew up, Mom," I explain, the familiar ache settling in my chest. "I'm forty-two now."

This seems to distress her further. "But I missed it," she says, her voice trembling. "I missed you growing up."

Caroline and I exchange pained looks over her bed. Our mother left when I was sixteen, unable to cope with our father's alcoholism and increasingly erratic behavior. She'd moved to Dallas, remarried, and started a new life. By the time she returned to Firelight Falls as a widow ten years ago, both Caroline and I were adults with lives of our own, and I was in Houston.

"You're here now," I assure her, squeezing her hand gently. "That's what matters."

She seems to accept this, though her eyes remain troubled. "Your father called," she blurts. "He's in trouble again."

My breath catches. It's almost exactly what she would have said twenty years ago, the night everything changed. "Dad's gone, Mom," I remind her softly. "He passed away five years ago."

"No," she insists, growing agitated. "He called. He needs money. Those men will hurt him if he doesn't pay."

Caroline steps in smoothly. "It's okay, Mom. Jake took care of it. Everything's fine now."

This seems to calm her. "You did?" she asks, looking at me with sudden clarity. "You fixed it?"

"I did," I say, the old weight of responsibility settling on my shoulders. "Everyone's safe."

She relaxes back against her pillows, apparently satisfied. "You're a good boy, Jake. Always trying to fix everything."

The simple assessment is so accurate, it's painful. Always trying to fix everything, to protect everyone, often at a steep personal cost.

Caroline and I stay until Mom falls asleep, then step out into the hallway to speak privately.

"This is the third time this week she's mentioned Dad's gambling debts," Caroline says, her voice low. "It's like her mind is stuck in that period."

"The worst period," I observe grimly.

"For all of us," she agrees. "But especially for you. You gave up everything to bail him out."

I shake my head. "Not everything."

"Annie," Caroline says softly. "That's what I meant."

We walk in silence to the parking lot, the evening air cool against my face after the warmth of the care facility.

"Are you seeing her tonight?" Caroline asks as we reach our vehicles.

"Dinner at eight," I say. "At the bakery."

She nods approvingly. "Good. Don't let Mom's confusion get to you. The past is the past, Jake. You did what you thought was right."

"Did I?" I ask, the question that's haunted me for twenty years finally voiced aloud. "Sometimes I wonder if I was just repeating Dad's pattern of making unilateral decisions that hurt the people who loved me."

Caroline's expression softens. "The difference is, you were trying to protect others. Dad was only ever protecting himself."

Her words offer some comfort, though the weight of the past still presses on me heavily. "I'll see you tomorrow," I tell her. "Spring Bloom committee meeting."

"Last one before the festival," she confirms. "Try not to look too lovesick when you see Annie. The gossips are already having a field day."

Despite my melancholy mood, I smile. "I'll do my best."

After a quick shower and change of clothes at home, I head back to the bakery, arriving just as the "Closed" sign is being turned. Annie waves me in, looking tired but satisfied after her busy reopening day.

"Perfect timing," she says. "I just finished the day's accounts."

"Successful day?" I ask, following her through the darkened bakery to the stairs leading to her apartment.

"Wildly," she confirms. "We sold out of almost everything by four o'clock."

Upstairs, her apartment is warm and inviting, the lingering scent of baking hanging sweetly in the air. Annie moves to the kitchen, pulling out menus from a drawer.

"Chinese or Italian?" she asks, holding up options.

"Whatever you're in the mood for," I reply, settling onto the stool at her kitchen counter.

She studies me for a moment, her head tilted slightly. "You okay? You seem... I don't know. Somewhere else."

I consider brushing it off, maintaining the light, carefully balanced dynamic we've established. But the raw emotion of the visit with my mother pushes me toward honesty.

"I visited my mother before coming here," I explain. "She's having a bad day. Confused about time, asking for my father."

Annie's face softens in understanding. "I'm sorry. That must be hard."

"It is," I admit. "Especially when she talks about his gambling debts, about the men who were threatening him. It brings everything back."

Annie sets the menus aside and comes around the counter, taking the stool beside mine. "Do you want to talk about it?"

After a moment, I decide to open up. "She said I was always trying to fix everything," I say, the words coming easier than expected. "And she's right. I've spent my whole life trying to fix my father's messes, protecting the people I care about, making things right."

"There's nothing wrong with that," Annie says softly.

"Isn't there?" I turn to face her fully. "Annie, I left you without a word because I thought I was protecting you. I made that decision for both of us, just like my father always made decisions for our family without considering what anyone else wanted or needed."

She's quiet for a moment, thinking over my words. "There's a difference," she says finally. "Your father made selfish choices. Yours, however misguided, came from a place of love."

"I've spent twenty years wondering if I became exactly what I feared most, someone who hurts the people they love."

Annie's hand covers mine on the counter, warm and steady. "You're not your father, Jake."

"How can you be so sure?" I ask, my voice rougher than intended. "I disappeared without a word. I left you wondering, worrying. For all you knew, I could have been—"

"Dead in a ditch somewhere?" she suggests, a hint of old anger flashing in her eyes. "Believe me, I considered every possibility. But here's the difference. Your father never came back. Never explained. Never apologized. You did."

Her words humble me. "Twenty years too late."

"Better late than never," she counters. "And you had a good reason, Jake. Not an excuse—there is no excuse for the way you left—but a reason I can understand."

Annie has always seen me clearly, even the parts of myself I try to hide.

"I missed you," I confess, the words inadequate for the ocean of feeling behind them. "Every day, every milestone. When I became a firefighter, when I got promoted, when Maddie was born, a part of me always wondered what you would think, what you would say."

Annie's eyes glisten slightly in the soft kitchen light. "I missed you too," she admits. "Even when I was angriest, I still missed my best friend."

Without thinking, I reach for her, pulling her into an embrace that feels like coming home. Her arms wrap around me without hesitation, her head fitting perfectly beneath my chin as it always has.

We stay like that for long moments, the comfort of our connection easing the strain of the day. When we finally pull apart, something has shifted.

"Chinese," Annie says abruptly.

I blink, momentarily confused. "What?"

"For dinner," she clarifies with a small smile. "I'm in the mood for Chinese food."

And just like that, the heavy moment transitions into something more manageable. We order food and settle on her sofa to wait for delivery, talking about everything and nothing.

When the food arrives, we eat at her small dining table, conversation flowing easily between us. I tell her about my years in the Houston Fire Department, about meeting Lisa, about the joy and heartbreak of our years together. Annie shares stories of building her bakery business, of the challenges and triumphs along the way.

"Did you ever think about leaving?" I ask as we finish our meal. "Firelight Falls, I mean. Going somewhere bigger?"

"Sometimes," she admits. "Especially right after you left. I thought about following you to Houston, tracking you down." A faint blush colors her cheeks at the admission.

"Why didn't you?" I ask, though I'm not sure I want to hear the answer.

"Grandma needed me," she says simply. "And I needed the stability, the familiarity of home after everything changed so suddenly."

I nod, understanding perfectly. "And later?"

"Later, I had built something here. Something that mattered." She shrugs. "It became harder to imagine leaving."

"Do you regret staying?" The question slips out before I can reconsider.

Annie is quiet for a long moment, considering. "No," she says finally. "I built a good life here. Made a difference in this community. Found purpose. I can't regret that."

I'm glad she found fulfillment, but I'm sorry I wasn't part of it.

"What about you?" she asks. "Do you regret leaving?"

It's the question I've been asking myself since returning to Firelight Falls. "I regret how I left," I say carefully. "The way I handled it. But if I hadn't gone to Houston, I wouldn't have become a firefighter. I wouldn't have met Lisa. Wouldn't have Maddie."

"And they were worth it," Annie says softly. Not a question, but an observation.

"They were," I confirm. "Are. But that doesn't mean I didn't lose something precious when I left you."

The naked honesty hangs between us, too big to ignore. Annie's eyes meet mine, something vulnerable and questioning in their depths.

"Jake," she begins, but whatever she might have said is interrupted by the shrill ring of my phone.

I check the screen with a frown. "It's the station," I tell her, answering quickly. "Colton."

Chief Williams's voice comes through, tense and urgent. "Chief, we've got a situation at the old Mason property on County Road 8. Structure fire, possibly with entrapment. Engine 1 is already en route, but given the location and conditions, we could use all hands."

"I'm on my way," I say, already rising from the table. "ETA ten minutes."

I end the call and turn to Annie, who's watching me with concern. "Fire?" she asks.

"The old Mason farmhouse," I confirm, grabbing my jacket. "I need to go."

She nods, understanding immediately. "Be careful."

"Always am," I promise. At the door, I pause. "Rain check on rest of the evening?"

"Of course." She walks me to the door. "Go be a hero, Chief Colton."

I touch her cheek briefly, wishing I could stay. "I'll call you when it's over."

The drive to the station is quick, my mind already shifting into emergency response mode. Within minutes, I'm in turnout gear, heading to the scene with Engine 2. The night sky is lit with an ominous orange glow long before we reach the property.

The old Mason farmhouse has been abandoned for years, but was recently purchased by a developer planning to renovate. It's fully engulfed when we pull up, flames shooting from windows and doors. Engine 1 is already on scene, firefighters deploying hoses and establishing a perimeter.

"Report," I call to Lieutenant Rodriguez as I approach the command point.

"Two-story structure, heavy fire on first floor, extending to second," he reports crisply. "Neighbor reported possible squatters inside, but we haven't confirmed occupancy. Structural integrity compromised. Roof could go any minute."

I assess the scene quickly, years of training and experience informing my decisions. "Set up defensive operations. No interior attack unless we confirm occupants. Protect the exposure to the barn."

The team moves with practiced efficiency, each firefighter executing their assigned role in our well-rehearsed emergency response plan. I coordinate with dispatch, requesting additional resources from neighboring departments.

We're making progress containing the blaze when a shout goes up from one of my men. "Movement! Second-floor window!"

I turn to see a figure at a window on the far side of the house, waving frantically. Even from this distance, I can see it's a teenager, maybe Maddie's age.

"Confirmed occupant," I announce over the radio. "Second floor, west side. Get a ladder up now."

Time narrows to a laser focus as we work to reach the trapped teen. The ladder goes up, but just as one of my firefighters climbs, there's an ominous cracking sound. The roof collapses, sending sparks and burning debris raining down.

"Fall back!" I order, watching with dread as the ladder becomes unusable, cut off by falling timbers.

The teen is still visible, now coughing as smoke pours from the window. There's no time for another approach from outside.

"I'm going in," I announce, pulling my mask into place.

"Chief, the structure's unstable," Rodriguez protests.

"We don't have a choice," I tell him. "Give me cover with the hose line. I'll go up through the east stairwell. It still looks intact."

Before anyone can argue further, I move toward the burning building, following the path of least resistance through the flames. Inside, heat and smoke create a disorienting maze, but I rely on my training, staying low, keeping in contact with walls.

The staircase is still standing, though flames lick at its edges. I climb quickly, radio crackling with concerned voices from my team outside. On the second floor, the smoke is thicker, reducing visibility to almost nothing.

"Fire department!" I call, my voice muffled by my mask. "Call out if you can hear me!"

A faint cough responds from my right. I follow the sound, crawling beneath the worst of the smoke, until I reach a room at the end of the hall. The teen is huddled by the window, a young girl with a soot-stained face and terror-filled eyes.

"I've got you," I tell her, reaching her side. "I'm going to get you out."

She nods, coughing violently. I assess her quickly for injuries, finding none that would prevent movement. "Can you walk?"

Another nod.

"Stay close to me," I instruct, helping her to her feet. "We're going back the way I came in."

We've barely left the room when a deafening crack sounds above us. I look up just in time to see the ceiling beams giving way. Without thinking, I push the girl forward and out of the path of the falling debris.

Pain explodes through my left shoulder and leg as something heavy pins me to the floor. The girl turns back, eyes wide with fear.

"Go!" I shout, pointing toward the staircase, now visible as a clearer area in the smoke. "Down the stairs! My team is outside!"

She hesitates, then runs as instructed. I activate my emergency beacon, alerting my team to my location. Through my radio, I confirm the girl is heading for the staircase, directing my firefighters to intercept her.

Then, I assess my situation. A support beam has fallen across my left side, trapping me in place. With my right arm, I try to leverage it off, but the angle is wrong, and pain shoots through my shoulder at the attempt.

The smoke is thickening, and the heat's intensifying. I control my breathing, preserving the oxygen in my tank while I wait for rescue. Through my radio, I hear confirmation that the girl has been found and evacuated. Relief flows through me, even as my situation grows more precarious.

Time blurs as smoke and pain cloud my senses. I think of Maddie, of my promise never to leave her alone after losing her mother. Of my mother, already confused and afraid. Of Caroline, who has carried so many of our family's burdens.

Of Annie, who I left once before without saying goodbye.

The thought galvanizes me. Not again. Not like this. With renewed determination, I work to free myself, ignoring the pain flaring through my injured side.

Just as darkness creeps at the edges of my vision, I hear voices, see the beams of flashlights cutting through the smoke. My team has reached me.

"Hold on, Chief," Rodriguez's voice comes through the haze. "We've got you."

Together, they lift the beam enough for me to be pulled free. Strong arms support me as we make our way through the burning building, down the compromised staircase, and finally out into the cool night air.

Outside, paramedics wait to assess me. Despite my protests, they insist on oxygen and an examination of my injuries. My shoulder is dislocated, my leg bruised but not broken. As they work, I maintain command, directing operations until the fire's contained, ensuring all my firefighters are accounted for.

The rescued teenager, who turns out to be a runaway from a neighboring town, has already been transported to the hospital for smoke inhalation. Her prognosis is good, according to the paramedics who treated her on the scene.

Only when the situation is fully under control, do I allow myself to be transported to the emergency room for treatment of my injuries. In the ambulance, as adrenaline fades and pain sharpens, I pull out my phone with my good hand and see multiple missed calls and texts from Caroline and Maddie. And from Annie.

News travels fast in Firelight Falls, especially when it involves the fire chief running into a burning building. I text Annie first.

> I'm okay. Dislocated shoulder, some bruises. Headed to ER for checkup. Call you later.

Her response comes immediately.

> Annie: I'm already at the hospital. Drove over when I heard. See you soon.

The message gives me more comfort than any pain medication could provide.

Some fires, I reflect as the ambulance speeds toward the hospital, change everything in their path, destroying what was to make way for what might be. The challenge is recognizing which flames to fight, and which to let burn their course.

Tonight, I fought. For a stranger's life, for my own, and for the chance to finally get things right with the woman who has held my heart for twenty years.

# Annie

Hospital waiting rooms are all the same—uncomfortable chairs, outdated magazines, televisions tuned to channels no one is watching. I've been sitting in the Firelight Falls Memorial Hospital emergency room for nearly an hour, waiting for news about Jake.

When Caroline called, her voice tight with worry, and told me Jake had been injured rescuing a teenager from a burning building, my heart nearly stopped. Even though she assured me his injuries weren't life-threatening, I grabbed my keys and drove to the hospital without a second thought.

"Ms. Barrett?"

I look up to see a young nurse in blue scrubs standing before me. "Yes?"

"Chief Colton is asking for you," she says with a smile. "He's in treatment room three. I can take you back."

I follow her through the automatic doors into the treatment area, my pulse quickening with each step. What will I find? How badly is he hurt?

The nurse pauses outside a curtained area. "Just so you're prepared, he's a bit banged up, but nothing too serious. Dislocated shoulder, some smoke inhalation, minor burns and lacerations."

I nod, grateful for the warning, and step through the curtain. Jake's sitting on the edge of an examination bed, bare-chested except for a sling supporting his left arm. His face is smudged with soot, and a nasty bruise is forming along his left side. But he's alive. Breathing. Looking at me with those impossibly blue eyes.

"You came," he says, his voice rough from smoke.

"Of course, I came," I reply, moving to his uninjured side. "You scared me half to death."

A small smile forms on his lips. "Just another day at the office."

"Running into burning buildings is not a normal office activity." I fight the urge to touch him, to physically confirm that he's really okay.

"For me, it is," he counters, then winces as he shifts position. "Though I usually come out with fewer souvenirs."

Before I can respond, a doctor enters. "Chief Colton, your X-rays look good. No fractures, just the dislocation, which we've reduced. You'll need to keep the shoulder immobilized for at least a week, preferably two." She glances at me. "Are you family?"

"She's—" Jake begins.

"Yes," I say firmly, cutting him off. "I'll be taking care of him."

The doctor nods, apparently satisfied. "Good. He'll need help for the first few days, at least. I'm prescribing pain medication and a muscle relaxant. He shouldn't drive while taking either." She hands me several papers. "Discharge instructions, prescriptions, and follow-up appointment information. Any questions?"

"What about work?" Jake asks.

"Administrative duties only for at least two weeks," the doctor says firmly. "No firefighting, no heavy lifting, nothing that could re-injure that shoulder. I've already spoken with your second-in-command, who assures me he can handle things."

Jake looks like he wants to argue, but a sharp look from me silences him. "He'll follow the doctor's orders," I promise.

After the doctor leaves, Jake raises an eyebrow at me. "So you're taking care of me?"

"Someone has to make sure you don't run into another burning building tomorrow," I say, helping him into a clean shirt that a firefighter had brought from the station. It's a challenge with the sling, but we manage. "Unless you'd prefer Caroline?"

Jake shudders dramatically. "God, no. She'd enjoy my helplessness too much."

"Then it looks like you're stuck with me." I gather his wallet, keys, and phone. "Someone told Maddie?"

He nods. "Caroline picked her up at a friend's house. They'll meet us at my place."

The discharge process takes another thirty minutes, during which I fill Jake's prescriptions at the hospital pharmacy. By the time we leave, it's past midnight, and fatigue is evident in the lines of Jake's face.

"My truck's over there," I tell him, guiding him toward the parking lot with a light touch on his good arm.

"How did you get my truck here?" he asks, confused.

"Not your truck," I clarify. "Mine."

Understanding dawns. "You're driving me home."

"Unless you plan to sprout wings, yes."

He smiles tiredly. "Lead the way."

The drive to Jake's house is quiet, both of us processing the events of the evening. I glance over occasionally, finding him looking out the window, his profile illuminated by passing streetlights. The enormity of what I could have lost just as we were finding our way back to each other weighs on me.

Jake's house is a modest craftsman-style home on the east side of town, with a wide front porch and neatly trimmed lawn. Lights glow in the windows, and Caroline's car is parked in the driveway. As I help Jake out of the truck, the front door opens.

"Dad!" Maddie rushes down the porch steps, stopping just short of throwing herself into her father's arms as she notices his sling. "Are you okay?"

"I'm fine, sweetheart," Jake assures her, using his good arm to pull her into a careful hug. "Just a little banged up."

Maddie turns to me, her expression a mixture of gratitude and curiosity. "Thanks for bringing him home, Ms. Barrett."

"Annie," I correct gently. "And you're welcome."

Caroline appears in the doorway, relief clear on her face. "It's about time you showed up," she calls to Jake. "I was about to send out a search party."

Inside, the house is warm and inviting, filled with comfortable furniture, family photos, and a distinct lack of frills.

"I've set up the downstairs guest room," Caroline tells us as we enter. "Figured stairs wouldn't be your friend tonight."

Jake nods gratefully. "Good thinking."

"And I've filled Maddie in on all the heroic details," she continues. "Though I'm sure the town rumor mill will have you single-handedly carrying an entire family of twelve out of the inferno by morning."

I smile. Caroline's ability to lighten even the most serious situations has always been one of her strengths.

"The teenager?" Jake asks. "Any updates?"

"Stable condition," Caroline reports. "Smoke inhalation, minor burns. They're keeping her overnight for observation, but she should make a full recovery. Parents are on their way."

Jake exhales in relief. "Good."

Maddie hovers nearby, attempting to hide her worry. I recognize the look of a child who's already lost one parent and is terrified of losing another.

"Why don't you help your dad get settled?" I suggest. "I'll make some tea."

She nods and guides Jake toward the guest room. Caroline follows me to the kitchen, watching as I fill a kettle and search for tea.

"Cabinet above the stove," she directs. "Mugs to the left."

I find the tea and set about preparing four cups. Caroline leans against the counter, observing me with undisguised interest.

"So," she says finally, "you and my brother."

I glance at her, wary of the direction this conversation might take. "What about us?"

"You rushed to the hospital the moment you heard."

"And?"

"And now you're in his kitchen, making tea, preparing to take care of him." She raises an eyebrow. "Seems like more than old friends catching up."

I focus on the task at hand, avoiding her perceptive gaze. "He was injured saving someone's life. I'd do the same for anyone."

"But he's not just anyone, is he?" Caroline presses.

The kettle whistles, saving me from having to respond immediately. I pour water into the mugs, the familiar ritual giving me time to collect my thoughts.

"It's complicated," I say finally, meeting her eyes.

"Love usually is," she replies simply.

The word hangs between us, both too large and too small for what exists between Jake and me. Is it love? Still? Again? Or something else entirely?

"I'm not trying to push," Caroline says. "But I've watched my brother carry the weight of his decision to leave for twenty years. I've never seen him as alive as he's been since coming back to you."

"He didn't come back for me," I remind her. "He came back for his mother. For Maddie."

"Keep telling yourself that," she says with a knowing smile. "But I know my brother. And I remember how he looked at you when you were kids. He's looking at you that way again."

Before I can respond, Jake and Maddie emerge from the guest room. Jake has changed into sweats and a t-shirt, the sling now over his clothes. He moves gingerly, doing his best to hide his pain with each careful step.

"Perfect timing," I say, handing Maddie two of the mugs. "Tea's ready."

We settle in the living room, and the conversation turns to safer topics like the Spring Bloom Festival preparations, Maddie's upcoming history project, and town gossip about who might be crowned Spring Queen. Gradually, the tension from the evening's emergency eases.

I watch Jake with his daughter, the gentle way he listens to her stories, his pride in her accomplishments. This is a side of him I'm just getting to know. Jake, the father, steady and supportive, a far cry from the reckless young man I once knew.

As the clock nears one in the morning, fatigue catches up with us. Caroline stands, stretching. "I should get home. Early court appearance tomorrow."

"I'll stay," I tell her. "Just for tonight, to make sure he takes his medication and doesn't try anything stupid."

Jake looks like he wants to protest but thinks better of it. "The guest room's yours," he tells me. "I can take the couch."

"Absolutely not," I counter. "You're taking the guest room. I'll sleep on the couch."

"Or," Maddie interjects, "Annie could take my room, and I could bunk with Aunt Caroline. She lives like three minutes away."

Before I can comment, Caroline pipes up, "Yeah, that would work. That way, I can keep an eye on her while you can take care of him."

Jake and I exchange glances, silently evaluating the suggestion.

"You don't have to leave, Maddie. Annie can just take my room," Jake says to Maddie.

"No, no. It's fine. I'm sure my room would be more comfortable for her," Maddie says in a hurry, looking pointedly at Caroline. "I have clothes at Aunt Caroline's from my last sleepover, and it's a weekend, anyway."

Decision made, Caroline and Maddie prepare to leave, gathering what Maddie needs for the night. As they head for the door, Maddie surprises me with a quick hug.

"Take care of him," she whispers. "He pretends he's fine when he's really not."

"I will," I promise, touched by how deeply she cares for her father.

After they leave, Jake and I are alone in the suddenly quiet house. He sits on the edge of the sofa, fatigue etched in every line of his body.

"You don't have to stay," he says, though his tone suggests he hopes I will. "I can manage."

"I know you can," I reply, collecting the empty mugs. "But you shouldn't have to. Besides, I promised Maddie."

A small smile touches his lips. "She likes you, you know. Says you're not what she expected."

"Oh?" I raise an eyebrow as I head toward the kitchen. "And what did she expect?"

Jake follows, leaning against the doorframe as I rinse the mugs. "I'm not entirely sure. But whatever she imagined when I told her about my childhood best friend, it wasn't the owner of her favorite bakery."

"You told her about me?" The revelation surprises me. "Even before coming back to Firelight Falls?"

He nods, his expression thoughtful. "She asked once about my first love. I told her the truth. That I met you when we were kids, that we grew up together, and that you were the most important person in my life before her mother."

"I'm sure that was a fun conversation."

"She was thirteen," Jake recalls. "Fascinated by the idea that people had lives before becoming parents. Lisa had just died, and Maddie was asking a lot of questions about love and loss. About whether it was worth the risk."

"What did you tell her?" I ask softly.

His eyes find mine across the kitchen. "That loving someone, truly loving them, is always worth the risk. Even when it hurts. Even when it ends. That I wouldn't trade the years with her mother, or the time with you, even knowing how painful losing that love would be."

The raw emotion in his voice steals my breath. For a moment, we stand frozen in his kitchen, the weight of twenty years and what might have been hanging between us.

"It's late," I say finally, breaking the spell. "And you need to take your medication before bed."

Jake nods, letting me change the subject. I help him with his pills, make sure he has water by the bed, and check that his sling's properly adjusted before saying goodnight.

"If you need anything, I'll be right upstairs," I tell him at the guest room door. "Don't be a hero. Again."

He smiles tiredly. "Yes, ma'am."

Upstairs, Maddie's room is exactly what I'd expect from a fifteen-year-old girl. Posters cover the walls, books are stacked on every surface, and clothes are draped over chairs. But there are also surprising touches. Framed photographs of what must be her mother, a collection of vintage vinyl records, a battered copy of "Pride and Prejudice" on the nightstand.

I find a t-shirt in a drawer that looks large enough to sleep in, change quickly, and slip between cool sheets that smell of laundry detergent and vaguely of teenage perfume. Exhaustion claims me quickly, pulling me into dreamless sleep.

Until a crash from downstairs jolts me awake.

I sit up, disoriented in the dark, until memory rushes back. Jake. I'm at Jake's house. And that sound...

Moving quickly, I grab my phone for light and hurry downstairs. I find Jake in the kitchen, a shattered glass on the floor around his bare feet, his expression a mixture of pain and frustration.

"Don't move," I warn, eyeing the broken glass. "You'll cut yourself."

"Too late," he admits, gesturing to his foot, where a small trickle of blood is already visible.

I sigh, locate the broom and dustpan in a nearby closet, and carefully sweep a path to him. "What were you doing?"

"Getting water," he says, sounding remarkably like a child caught doing something forbidden. "My pain medication wore off."

"Why didn't you call me?" I ask, guiding him to a chair well away from the glass.

"It's three in the morning," he points out. "I didn't want to wake you."

I shoot him a look as I finish sweeping up the glass. "That worked out well."

Once the floor is clean, I turn my attention to his injured foot. The cut is small but needs cleaning. I find the first aid kit under the bathroom sink and return to kneel before him, taking his foot in my hands.

"This might sting," I warn, applying antiseptic.

Jake hisses slightly but doesn't pull away. "Sorry for waking you," he says, watching as I work. "I'm not used to having help."

"Well, get used to it. At least for the next few days."

I place a small bandage over the cut, my hands lingering perhaps longer than necessary on his ankle. When I look up, Jake is watching me with an expression I can't quite decipher.

"Annie," he breathes.

"Let me get your medication," I interrupt, rising quickly. "And some water. In a plastic cup this time."

I busy myself gathering what he needs, acutely aware of his gaze following me around the kitchen. There's something deeply intimate about the moment—me in a baggy tee, him in sleepwear, tending to his wounds like it's the most natural thing in the world.

"Here," I say, returning with water and pills. "These should help."

Jake takes them without argument, then sets the cup aside. "Thank you."

"It's just a bandage," I mumble.

"Not just for that," he clarifies. "For coming to the hospital, driving me home, staying... For caring, even after everything that happened between us."

"That's what friends do," I say, though the word 'friends' feels inadequate for what we are to each other.

"Is that what we are? Friends?" Jake's question is gentle.

I meet his eyes in the dim kitchen light. "I don't know what we are anymore," I admit. "But I know I care about what happens to you. I know I was terrified when Caroline called about the fire. And I know I'm not ready to put a label on any of this yet."

He nods. "Fair enough."

"Can you make it back to bed?" I ask, changing the subject.

"I think so," he says, standing carefully. "Though I wouldn't mind help."

I offer my arm, and he leans on me slightly as we walk back to the guest room. At the door, he hesitates.

"Stay?" he asks, then quickly clarifies. "Just to talk for a while. The pain medication makes me restless before it knocks me out."

I should say no. Should return to Maddie's room, and maintain the careful distance we've established. But the vulnerability in his request, and perhaps my desire for connection after the fear of almost losing him, weaken my resolve.

"For a little while," I agree.

I sit cross-legged at the foot of his bed while he props himself against the headboard. There's space between us, but the quiet comfort of simply being here together remains.

"Tell me about the bakery," Jake says. "How it started."

So I do, sharing the story of how Martha's Kitchen began. How I used my grandmother's recipes, my business degree, and took a wild leap of faith buying the old hardware store and converting it into something new. Jake listens intently, asking questions at just the right moments.

Gradually, our conversation drifts to books we've read, places we've traveled, lessons we've learned. It's like rediscovering an old friend while simultaneously getting to know a new one.

"I kept a box," Jake says suddenly during a lull in conversation. "Letters I wrote to you over the years. Things I wanted to tell you but couldn't."

The confession startles me. "You wrote me letters?"

He nods, his expression open, vulnerable. "Dozens of them. Every time something important happened. Every time I missed you more than usual. When I got my firefighter certification. When I met Lisa, and when Maddie was born."

"You never sent them."

"No," he admits. "At first, because I was trying to give you the clean break I thought you deserved. Later, because it had been too long, and I didn't know how to bridge that gap."

"Do you still have them?" I ask, curious.

"Yes," he says . "They're yours, if you ever want to read them."

The offer hangs between us, as intimate as a touch. "I don't know if I'm ready for that," I tell him honestly.

"That's okay," he says. "They're not going anywhere."

Like the letters, I realize, parts of who we were have been frozen in time—unchanged, patiently waiting while the rest of us moved forward. The real challenge now is figuring out how those fragments fit with who we are today.

I notice Jake struggling to keep his eyes open, the medication finally taking effect. "I should let you sleep," I say, moving to stand.

"Annie," he murmurs, already half-dreaming. "I'm glad you're here."

"Me too," I whisper, though I'm not sure he hears me.

I return to Maddie's room, but sleep doesn't come. My mind circles with thoughts of Jake, of letters he never sent, of what might have been and what could be. Eventually, I drift into a restless sleep, dreaming of burning buildings and rescue ladders that never quite reach high enough.

# Jake

I WAKE TO SUNLIGHT streaming through unfamiliar curtains, momentarily disoriented before remembering—the fire, the hospital, Annie bringing me home. Annie staying overnight.

Pain radiates from my shoulder as I sit up, a reminder of yesterday's rescue and its consequences. The clock on the nightstand reads 9:17—later than I've slept in years.

The house is quiet as I make my way to the bathroom. Every movement requires calculation now, a mental mapping of how to accomplish simple tasks with one arm immobilized. Brushing teeth. Washing my face. Each minor victory feels disproportionately satisfying.

When I emerge, the scent of coffee and something sweet leads me to the kitchen. Annie stands at the stove, still in the oversized t-shirt she slept in, paired now with her jeans from yesterday. Her hair's pulled into a messy bun, and she hums softly as she flips what appear to be pancakes.

For a moment, I just watch her, struck by the rightness of the scene. How many mornings had I imagined exactly this during our years apart? Annie in my kitchen, making breakfast, at home in my space.

"Good morning," I say finally.

She turns, a spatula in hand, and smiles. "You're up. How's the shoulder?"

"Reminding me it exists," I admit, moving to the coffeemaker. "But manageable."

"I found pancake mix in the pantry," she explains. "Hope that's okay."

"More than okay," I assure her, pouring coffee with my good hand. "I didn't expect breakfast service."

"Consider it part of the Annie Barrett home healthcare package," she says lightly. "Coffee, pancakes, and unnecessary commentary on your patient compliance."

I smile, settling carefully onto a kitchen stool. "And how am I doing on that front?"

"To be determined," she replies, transferring pancakes to a plate. "But climbing out of bed for water in the middle of the night wasn't a promising start."

As we eat, conversation flows easily between us. Annie tells me about the bakery's weekend specials, her plans for festival preparation, and a challenging wedding cake order. I share stories about the fire department's community outreach programs, and my mother's good days at Sunset Pines.

It feels normal. Comfortable. As if we've been sharing breakfast for years rather than rebuilding bridges between us with careful, measured steps.

"I called Chief Williams this morning," Annie mentions, gathering our empty plates. "Let him know you're following doctor's orders. He's handling the incident reports and said not to worry about anything until Monday."

"You called my second-in-command?" I ask, surprised.

"Someone had to. And your phone's been buzzing with messages since dawn. I figured that would be one less thing you needed to deal with."

"Thank you," I say, touched by the thoughtfulness of the gesture.

"Caroline's stopping by around noon with Maddie and some groceries. I made a list of things you might need for the next few days."

"You've thought of everything," I say.

"I run a bakery," she reminds me. "Planning is part of the job description."

As she loads the dishwasher, I notice her glancing at the clock. "Do you need to get to the bakery?" I ask.

"Lana's handling things today," she says. "I called her earlier."

"You don't have to stay," I tell her, though I hope she will. "I can manage."

Annie gives me a skeptical look. "Can you? You can't even put on a shirt properly with that sling."

She has a point. "At least let me pay you back somehow."

"Keep yourself out of burning buildings for the next few weeks, and we'll call it even," she says, shaking her head. "You nearly gave me a heart attack."

We move to the living room, where Annie helps me settle on the couch with pillows supporting my injured shoulder. She finds the remote, turns on a cooking show, and sits beside me, leaving a careful distance between us.

"I have a confession," she says after a while.

I glance over, curious. "What's that?"

"I was furious with you when Caroline called about the fire." Her eyes remain on the television, but I can see the tension in her profile. "Not just worried. Angry."

"Why?" I ask, though I think I already know.

"Because you ran into that building," she says, confirming my suspicion. "You risked your life. You could have..." She stops, swallowing hard.

"It's my job, Annie," I say keeping my voice soft and even.

"I know that." She turns to face me, her eyes fierce with emotion. "Intellectually, I understand that's what firefighters do. But knowing you were in danger, that you could have died in that house..." She shakes her head. "It brought everything back. The day you disappeared. The not knowing. The fear."

Now I understand. This isn't just about last night's fire. It's about history threatening to repeat itself.

"I came back," I remind her softly. "And I always will, if I have any say in the matter."

"But sometimes you don't have a say. And that's what scares me."

That she cares enough to be scared, that she's invested enough in my presence to fear my absence, sends warmth spreading through my chest.

"Annie," I begin, not entirely sure what I'm going to say, only knowing I need to reassure her somehow.

But the doorbell interrupts whatever might have followed. Annie stands, smoothing her shirt. "That's probably Caroline and Maddie."

The moment breaks, and the conversation's left unfinished as Annie goes to answer the door. Caroline's voice carries in from the entryway, followed by Maddie's quick chatter and Annie's warm hello.

They enter the living room laden with grocery bags and, in Maddie's case, an enormous bouquet of spring flowers.

"Hey, hero," Caroline greets me. "You look better than expected."

"These are for you," Maddie says, handing the flowers to Annie. "For taking care of Dad."

Annie accepts them with a surprised smile. "Thank you, Maddie. That's very thoughtful."

"It was Aunt Caroline's idea," Maddie admits, then turns to me. "How are you feeling, Dad?"

"Better," I assure her. "Annie's been taking good care of me."

"I bet she has," Caroline murmurs, earning herself a warning look from me.

The rest of the morning slips by easily. Caroline puts away groceries, giving me a hard time about my embarrassingly empty fridge. Maddie shows Annie her photography portfolio, explaining each shot with excitement. I sit on the couch and watch them, surprised by how easily Annie fits in with us.

Around noon, Annie announces she should head home. "I've imposed on your Saturday long enough," she says, gathering her purse. "And I really should check on the bakery. Make sure Lana hasn't burned it down again."

"Too soon," I protest, but I'm smiling.

"I'll just head out," Annie says, already reaching for her keys.

Caroline pulls Maddie into the kitchen with an excuse to refill my water, leaving the two of us alone for a moment.

"Thank you," I say.

"You already said that," she reminds me.

"It bears repeating."

She studies me for a moment, her expression softening. "You're welcome. Try to rest this weekend, okay? Doctor's orders."

"Yes, ma'am," I agree. "Will I see you tomorrow?"

It comes out quieter than I meant it to, exposing just how much I've enjoyed her being here.

"I could stop by after the bakery closes," she offers. "Bring dinner."

"I'd like that," I tell her, not bothering to hide my eagerness.

Annie says her goodbyes as Caroline and Maddie return to the living room. At the door, she pauses, then leans in and brushes a soft kiss against my cheek.

"Rest," she whispers, then she's gone.

I touch my cheek, still warm from her kiss, as I close the door. Turning, I find Maddie and Caroline watching me with barely concealed interest.

"Well, I'll leave you to it. I need to prepare for court." Caroline hugs Maddie, winks at me from across the room, and slips out the door.

"So," Maddie says, drawing out the word. "Annie, huh?"

"Annie what?" I ask, playing dumb.

My daughter rolls her eyes. "Please. I'm fifteen, not blind. You look at her like she hung the moon."

"Is it that obvious?" I ask, not bothering to deny it.

"To everyone except maybe Annie," she confirms. "Though from that goodbye kiss, I'd say she's catching on."

I ease my way back to the couch, considering how to approach this conversation. Maddie follows, curling up at the opposite end.

"Does it bother you?" I ask finally. "The idea of me and Annie?"

Maddie considers this seriously. "No," she says after a moment. "I like her. She's not what I expected, but in a good way. And she obviously cares about you."

"But?" I prompt, sensing there's more.

"But Mom hasn't been gone that long," she says. "Sometimes it feels like... like I'm the only one who still misses her every day."

Her honesty breaks my heart. I reach for her hand with my good arm, squeezing gently. "I miss her too, sweetheart. Every single day. That'll never change."

"I know," she acknowledges. "I know that. But feelings aren't always logical."

"No, they're not," I agree. "And there's no timeline for grief. No right or wrong way to process it."

"Yeah, the counselor told me that, too." She offers a small smile. "I want you to be happy, Dad, really. And if Annie makes you happy, then I'm okay with that. I just need to know that Mom still matters."

"Your mother will always matter," I assure her fiercely. "She gave me you. You're the best thing in my life. Nothing and no one could ever change how important she was, how much I loved her."

Maddie nods, blinking back tears. "Okay."

"And for what it's worth," I add gently, "whatever happens or doesn't happen with Annie, it doesn't diminish what your mom and I had. Different loves can exist in a heart. They don't cancel each other out."

"Like how I can love photography and still love soccer?" she suggests, attempting to lighten the mood.

I smile, grateful for her resilience. "Something like that."

We spend the rest of the day watching movies, ordering pizza for dinner, and carefully avoiding any more emotional landmines. By evening, I'm tired, my body reminding me that despite the comfortable day, I'm still recovering from significant trauma.

As Maddie helps me settle into the guest room for the night, she hesitates at the door. "Dad?"

"Hmm?"

"I'm glad you helped that girl," she says. "Even though you got hurt. It's what you do—help people, save them. It's who you are."

"Thank you, sweetheart."

"Just try not to get yourself killed doing it," she adds with forced casualness. "I kind of need you around."

"I'll do my very best."

After she leaves, I lie awake for a long time, reflecting on the day's conversations. Maddie's honest concerns about her mother's place in our lives. Annie's fear of losing me, of history repeating itself. I hope that somehow, against all odds, I might be given a second chance at the love I walked away from twenty years ago.

A firebreak, in firefighting, is a gap that stops a wildfire from spreading. I think life needs those too—empty spaces where we can step back, breathe, and keep emotions from burning out of control.

This injury slowed everything down, giving me room to see more clearly. To sift through the mess of old hurts and misunderstandings and figure out what still matters.

Just before sleep takes me, I remember Annie's kiss. Soft, tentative, full of something that felt like hope. Not a clean slate, but a spark—proof that even long-cooled embers can catch again, if tended with care.

# Annie

The Spring Bloom Festival is only three days away, and Firelight Falls has transformed into a flurry of activity. Main Street blooms with fresh paint and hanging flower baskets, vendor booths are being constructed in the town square, and the waterfall park—where the lantern release will take place—is decked with twinkling lights that reflect off the cascading water.

The bakery has been equally chaotic, with special orders flooding in for festival-themed treats and the baking contest preparations reaching fever pitch. I've barely had time to breathe, let alone think about my relationship with Jake.

Yet somehow, he's been constantly present in my thoughts. The memory of his injured body on the hospital bed, and the vulnerability in his eyes as I tended his foot in the middle of the night. The warmth of his cheek beneath my lips when I said goodbye.

"Earth to Annie." Lana waves a hand in front of my face, pulling me from my thoughts. "The festival committee meeting starts in twenty minutes. Are you sure you don't want me to go instead?"

I shake my head, returning to the present. "No, I'll go. I have the final contest details to review with Mayor Wilson."

"And it has nothing to do with seeing a certain fire chief?" Lana teases.

"He won't be there," I tell her, untying my apron. "Still on restricted duty."

It's been four days since Jake's injury, and though we've spoken daily on the phone, our dinner was postponed when Maddie came down with a stomach bug. I've tried not to feel disappointed, reminding myself that Jake's primary responsibility is to his daughter, as it should be.

"Well, that explains the moping," Lana observes, tucking a stray curl behind her ear.

"I'm not moping," I protest, though I suspect my tone gives me away.

"Mmm-hmm." Lana gives me a side eye. "Just go to your meeting. I'll finish closing up."

The town hall is bustling when I arrive, committee members chatting in small groups before the formal meeting begins. Caroline spots me and waves me over to where she stands with Ben Martinez.

"Annie," she greets me warmly. "How's the baking contest coming along?"

"Twenty-five contestants, four categories, and more pies than Firelight Falls has seen in a decade," I report. "We're ready."

"Glad to hear it," Ben says. "I've been practicing my judging face." He shows an exaggerated expression of contemplation that makes both Caroline and me laugh.

"Very judicial," Caroline approves. "Speaking of judging, have you heard from my brother today?"

The abrupt shift catches me off guard. "Not since this morning. Why?"

"He had his follow-up appointment with the orthopedic specialist," she explains. "I've been in court all day and haven't checked in."

A flicker of concern ignites in my chest. "He didn't mention the appointment."

"Typical Jake," Caroline sighs. "Always downplaying the important stuff."

Mayor Wilson calls the meeting to order before I can respond, and we take our seats around the conference table. We go over final security measures, schedule confirmations, and volunteer assignments. I present the baking contest logistics, distribute judging criteria to the panel members, and confirm the awards ceremony timing.

Throughout it all, part of my mind remains fixed on Jake. Why hadn't he mentioned the appointment? Was he trying to shield me from worry, or simply not burden me with his problems? Either way, the omission stings slightly, a reminder that despite our growing closeness, there are still boundaries between us.

After the meeting adjourns, I check my phone, finding no messages. Making a decision, I approach Caroline.

"Do you think he'd mind if I stopped by?" I ask. "Just to check in about the appointment."

A knowing smile curves her lips. "I think he'd be upset if you didn't."

With that, I head to my truck and drive the now-familiar route to Jake's house. The spring evening is perfect. Mild air scented with blooming jasmine, the sky painted in watercolor shades of pink and gold as the sun begins its descent... It's breathtaking.

Jake's truck is in the driveway, alongside Maddie's bicycle. I hesitate before approaching the door, suddenly uncertain of my welcome. This isn't a planned visit. What if he's resting? What if Maddie is still sick?

Before I can second-guess myself anymore, the door opens, and Jake stands there, his left arm still in a sling but otherwise looking much better than when I'd last seen him.

"Were you going to stand there all night?" he asks, a smile softening the question.

"How did you know I was here?" I counter, moving toward the porch.

"Small town fire chief," he reminds me. "I have spies everywhere. Also, I saw your truck pull up from the kitchen window."

His humor puts me at ease. "I heard you had a doctor's appointment today. I wanted to check how it went."

"Caroline?" he guesses, stepping aside to let me enter.

"She mentioned it at the committee meeting," I say, and shrug my shoulders to hide the sting of hurt. "You didn't tell me."

Jake leads me to the kitchen, where something savory simmers on the stove. "I didn't want to bother you with it. You've been swamped with festival preparations."

"It wouldn't have been a bother," I tell him, unable to keep a hint of hurt from my voice.

He turns to face me, his expression softening. "You're right. I should have told you. Old habits, I guess."

"What habits?" I ask, settling onto a stool at the counter.

"Handling things alone," he admits. "Not wanting to burden others with my problems."

His honesty soothes me. "So how did it go? The appointment."

"Better than expected," he says, stirring whatever's on the stove. "The shoulder's healing well. I should be able to start physical therapy next week. Light duty at the station starting Monday."

"That's good news," I say, genuinely relieved. "Where's Maddie?"

"Sleepover at a friend's house," Jake explains. "She's feeling much better. The twenty-four-hour bug passed quickly, thankfully."

I glance around the empty kitchen, the implication sinking in. We're alone. No interruptions, no distractions, just the two of us in the quiet intimacy of his home.

"Have you eaten?" Jake asks. "I made enough stew for an army. Old family recipe."

"I haven't," I admit. "The bakery was busy, and then the meeting..."

"Stay for dinner," he says, more statement than question. "Please."

How can I refuse when he looks at me like that, blue eyes warm with invitation? "I'd like that."

Jake smiles, clearly pleased by my acceptance. "Great. It's almost ready."

I watch as he moves around the kitchen, surprisingly adept even with the sling. "Can I help with anything?"

"You can pour the lemonade," he suggests, nodding toward a pitcher on the counter. "Glasses are in the cabinet to your left."

We work in comfortable silence. I set the table while Jake puts the finishing touches on dinner. "This smells amazing," I say as he ladles beef stew into bowls. "I didn't know you could cook."

"I had to learn after Lisa passed," he explains, joining me at the table. "Takeout gets old pretty fast, and Maddie deserved proper meals."

I take a bite, savoring the rich flavors. "This is definitely proper. Better than proper."

Jake looks pleased with the compliment. "My mother's recipe. One of the few positive things she left behind when she took off."

The casual reference to his mother's abandonment catches me by surprise. Jake rarely spoke of it, even when we were young. "How's she doing?" I ask carefully. "Your mom?"

"Some days are better than others," he says, his expression growing somber. "Her illness is progressing. The doctors say it's not unusual for traumatic memories to surface more frequently as the disease advances."

"Like your father's gambling debts," I surmise.

He nods. "And leaving us. I think she carries a lot of guilt about that."

"She left to protect herself," I observe.

"Yeah," Jake agrees. "But in doing so, she left Caroline and me unprotected. She made a choice to save herself at our expense."

The parallel to his own choice twenty years ago hangs unspoken between us. I take a sip of lemonade, considering my response.

"People make impossible choices sometimes," I say finally. "Especially when they're scared, or desperate, or trying to shield those they love from harm."

Jake's eyes meet mine, recognition flaring in their depths. "Some choices haunt you forever," he says. "No matter how necessary they seemed."

"And some choices can be explained and forgiven."

A tentative hope dawns in his expression. "Are we still talking about my mother?"

"I'm not sure," I admit honestly.

We fall silent, the weight of unspoken feelings filling the space between us. Outside, twilight deepens into evening, stars beginning to emerge in the sky.

"Would you like to sit outside?" Jake suggests after we finish eating. "It's a beautiful night."

I help him clear the table, refusing his attempts to wash dishes. "They can wait," I insist. "Doctor's orders."

Jake's back porch overlooks a small, neatly kept garden. Two Adirondack chairs face the horizon, where the last traces of sunset linger.

We settle into them, glasses in hand, the mild spring air enveloping us like a gentle embrace.

"I've missed this," Jake says after a comfortable silence. "Quiet evenings, pleasant conversation. Adult company."

"Being a single parent can't be easy," I observe.

"It has its challenges," he acknowledges. "But Maddie makes it worthwhile. She's the best of Lisa and me combined."

"She seems like a remarkable young woman," I say. "You've done a good job with her."

Jake's smile is soft, touched with pride. "I try. Some days I feel like I'm making it up as I go along."

"Isn't that what all parents do?" I suggest.

"Probably," he agrees. "Did you ever think about it? Having children?"

The question catches me off guard, though it shouldn't. It's a natural topic between old friends approaching middle age, reminiscing about paths taken and not taken.

"Sometimes," I admit. "There was a man about eight years ago. David. We were together for nearly three years, engaged for one. We talked about children."

Jake's expression remains neutral, though I notice his hand tighten slightly around his glass. "What happened?"

"He got a job offer in Seattle," I say. "A once-in-a-lifetime opportunity. He wanted me to go with him, sell the bakery, start over."

"But you couldn't leave Firelight Falls," Jake surmises.

"I couldn't leave my grandmother," I correct. "Her health was already declining. And yes, the bakery was important to me. I'd built something here, something that mattered."

"So he left," Jake says, a hint of judgment in his tone.

"We both made our choices," I remind him. "Neither of us was willing to sacrifice what mattered most. It was painful, but ultimately the right decision for both of us."

Jake's quiet for a moment, processing this. "Do you regret it? Not going with him?"

I consider the question seriously. "No," I say finally. "I loved David, but not enough to abandon everything else I loved. If it had been the right relationship, the right person, we would've found a way to make it work despite the obstacles."

The implications of my statement hover between us, unspoken but unmistakable. Jake and I had also faced obstacles. He left. What did that say about what we had been to each other?

"Lisa and I almost divorced once," Jake says abruptly, as if reading my thoughts. "Early in our marriage, before Maddie. I was working long hours at the fire department, taking extra shifts, burning myself out. She felt neglected, abandoned in a city where she had few friends."

I listen silently, sensing he needs to share this piece of his past.

"We separated for three months," he continues. "During that time, I realized what I was doing—working myself to exhaustion to avoid dealing with emotions, with connections. The same pattern I'd fallen into after leaving Firelight Falls. After leaving you."

His directness takes my breath away. "What happened?" I ask softly.

"I got help," he says simply. "Started therapy. Learned how to talk about feelings instead of running from them. Learned how to be present, to let people in." He meets my eyes directly. "Lisa took me back. We rebuilt our marriage, stronger than before. She taught me how to love without fear."

The raw honesty of his confession surprises me. I never knew this reflective, emotionally aware Jake. A man willing to acknowledge his flaws and work to overcome them.

"She sounds like a remarkable woman," I say sincerely.

"She was," Jake agrees. "And one of the things I loved most about her was her capacity for forgiveness. Her belief that people can change. That they can become better versions of themselves."

"I believe that too," I tell him, meaning it. The evidence is sitting right beside me. The reckless boy I once loved is now a thoughtful man, shaped by both joy and heartbreak into someone of depth and substance.

Jake reaches across the space between our chairs, his hand finding mine in the gathering darkness. "Annie," he says, his voice low and serious. "These past weeks, being around you again, talking like this... it's made me realize how much I've missed you."

My heart races. "Jake—"

"You don't have to say anything," he continues. "I know we're still figuring this out, whatever this is between us. I just wanted you to know that I see you. Not just the girl I left behind, but the incredible woman sitting beside me right now."

Emotions well up, too complex to name—gratitude, fear, and hope for what might still be possible between us.

"I see you too," I whisper. "The man you've become. The father, the firefighter, the son, the friend. All of it."

His fingers tighten around mine, a connection more powerful than words. We sit like that for a long time, holding hands beneath the starlit Texas sky, the distant sound of the waterfall filling the silence between us.

Eventually, the cooling night air sends us back inside. I help Jake build a fire in the small hearth, its warm glow casting dancing shadows across the living room. We settle on the couch, closer now than we might have a few days ago.

"Tell me about the letters," I say suddenly, surprising myself with the request. "The ones you wrote but never sent."

"What do you want to know?"

"What did you write?" I ask. "What did you want to tell me all those years?"

He's quiet for a moment, gathering his thoughts. "The first ones were full of explanations, apologies. Details about my father's debts, the men who were threatening him, my plan to earn enough money to pay them off."

I nod, encouraging him to continue.

"Later, it became a kind of journal. Things I wanted to share with you—my firefighter training, my first major rescue, moving into my apartment. I wrote to you the night I met Lisa, trying to understand why I felt both drawn to her and guilty about it, as if I were betraying you somehow."

I'm touched. "And after that?"

"Less frequent, but deeper," he says. "I wrote when Maddie was born. About how holding her reminded me of everything good and pure in the world, and how terrified I was of failing her. I wrote when Lisa was diagnosed, when treatments failed, when we knew the end was coming."

Tears prick at my eyes, imagining Jake pouring his heart out in letters I would never read. "The most recent?" I ask, my voice barely above a whisper.

"Two weeks before I moved back to Firelight Falls," he says. "Trying to sort through my feelings about returning, about possibly seeing you again. Wondering if you were happy, if you were married, if you'd long since moved on. Hoping you had, for your sake, and selfishly hoping you hadn't, for mine."

The raw vulnerability of his confession steals my breath. "Why keep writing all those years, knowing I'd never read them?"

Jake looks away, considering how to answer. "In the beginning, it was a way of holding onto you, of maintaining some connection, even if one-sided. Later, I think it became a habit, a way of processing my experiences through the lens of 'what would Annie think about this?' And eventually, they became a record of my journey. Who I was, who I was becoming, how much of that was still shaped by having loved you."

"You said they're mine, if I want them," I remind him, heart pounding.

"They are," he confirms. "Whenever you're ready. If you're ever ready."

"I think I am," I whisper. "Not tonight, but soon."

Jake nods, understanding in his eyes. "They'll be here when you are."

The fire crackles softly in the hearth, casting a warm glow over us both. Outside, a gentle rain falls, drumming against the roof in a soothing rhythm.

"It's getting late," I say reluctantly. "I should probably go."

"It's pouring. And you've had a long day. Stay."

The invitation hangs between us, fraught with possibility and unspoken boundaries. "Jake—"

"You can have the guest room," he clarifies quickly. "No pressure, no expectations. Just concern for your safety on wet roads."

"Okay," I agree. "But I don't have anything to sleep in."

"That can be arranged," he says with a slight smile. "Though you seemed comfortable enough in Maddie's t-shirt last time."

The memory of that night brings warmth to my cheeks. "That'll work," I say.

Jake stands, offering his hand to help me up from the couch. "I'll find you something to wear and show you to the guest room."

I follow him upstairs, where he retrieves a soft cotton t-shirt and toothbrush still in its packaging. "Bathroom's across the hall," he tells me. "There are towels in the cabinet if you want to shower."

"Thank you," I say, accepting the items.

He hesitates, something unspoken in his eyes. "Annie—"

"Yes?"

Instead of answering, he takes a step closer, his good hand coming up to gently cup my cheek. "May I?" he whispers, his intention clear.

My heart thunders in my chest, anticipation and nervousness mingling in equal measure. I nod, unable to form words.

Jake leans in slowly, giving me every opportunity to pull away. When his lips finally meet mine, the contact is feather-light. I respond instinctively, my hands coming to rest on his chest as I return the kiss with equal gentleness.

It's nothing like the passionate embraces of our youth, yet somehow more profound. There's history in this kiss, knowledge of loss and separation, appreciation for the miracle of second chances. It's tender, careful, a beginning.

When we part, Jake's eyes search mine, looking for reassurance. "Okay?" he asks softly.

"More than okay," I whisper.

His smile is radiant, relieved. "Good," he says simply. "Good."

We stand there, neither willing to break the moment, until I finally step back. "Goodnight, Jake."

"Goodnight, Annie," he responds, his voice warm with promise. "Sleep well."

I brush my teeth, change into the borrowed T-shirt, and slide beneath the cool sheets. But my mind won't settle. It keeps circling back to the kiss, and what it could mean from here.

Yet somehow, lulled by the gentle rain against the window and the lingering warmth of Jake's lips on mine, I drift into the most peaceful sleep I've had in years.

# Jake

THE MORNING AFTER KISSING Annie Barrett for the first time in twenty years, I wake with a sense of lightness I haven't felt since before Lisa's illness. Outside, the rain has cleared, leaving behind that particular freshness that follows a spring shower—clean air, sparkling droplets on leaves, the sense of renewal.

Last night feels like a dream, fragile and precious—her hand in mine beneath the stars, the soft yielding of her lips against mine.

In the kitchen, I start coffee brewing, then check my phone. A text from Maddie confirms she's having breakfast with her friend's family and will be home by noon. That gives me a few hours alone with Annie, a thought that both exhilarates and terrifies me.

I hear her before I see her—soft footsteps on the stairs, a slight pause at the kitchen doorway. When I turn, the sight of her steals my breath. She stands there in yesterday's jeans and my borrowed t-shirt, her hair tousled from sleep, her face bare of makeup. She's never looked more beautiful.

"Good morning," I say, trying to keep my voice casual. "Coffee?"

"Please," she replies, moving into the kitchen. "Did you sleep well?"

It's such a normal question, yet loaded with subtext after last night's kiss. "Better than I have in a long time," I tell her honestly. "You?"

"Like a rock," she admits, accepting the mug I offer. "Something about the rain."

"Something about the company," I suggest, testing the waters.

A blush tinges her cheeks, but she doesn't look away. "Maybe that too."

We stand there, sipping coffee, watching each other over the rims of our mugs. There's a newness to our interaction this morning, a heightened awareness of each gesture, each glance.

"About last night," I begin, needing to address the kiss directly.

"Yes?" She sets her mug down, giving me her full attention.

"I don't regret it," I say firmly. "Not for a second. But I want you to know that I understand if you need time, if you're not sure about... where this is going. I've had twenty years to think about what I lost when I left. You've had less than a month to adjust to me being back."

Annie's expression softens at my words. "I appreciate that," she says. "And you're right. This is all happening quickly. Part of me feels like we should slow down, be cautious, protect ourselves."

"And the other part?" I ask, holding my breath.

"The other part remembers that life can change in an instant," she says, her eyes serious. "That burning buildings collapse, that people we love can be diagnosed with terminal illnesses, that tomorrow is never guaranteed."

The simple wisdom strikes deep. "So where does that leave us?"

Annie moves closer, setting her coffee aside. "I think it leaves us here," she says, her voice soft but certain. "Two people with a complicated history and an uncertain future, trying to be honest about what they feel in the present."

"And what do you feel?" I ask, my heart hammering against my ribs.

She meets my gaze steadily. "Scared. Hopeful. Confused. Certain. Everything all at once."

"That sounds about right," I acknowledge with a small smile.

"What about you?" she asks. "What do you feel?"

I consider the question seriously, wanting to give her the honesty she deserves. "Grateful," I say finally. "For this second chance I never thought I'd have. Determined not to waste it. And yes, terrified of making another mistake, of hurting you again."

"I'm not twenty-two anymore," she reminds me gently. "I'm stronger now. More resilient."

"I know," I tell her. "I see that every day in how you run your business, care for your grandmother, and support your friends. You've built a life to be proud of, Annie."

"So have you," she counters. "Despite everything, or maybe because of it, you've become someone I admire. A good father, a dedicated firefighter, a man who takes responsibility for his actions."

Her praise sends warmth spiraling through my stomach. "So where do we go from here?" I ask.

Annie considers this, her green eyes thoughtful. "Forward," she says simply. "One day at a time. No promises we can't keep, no expectations we can't meet. Just... seeing what happens next."

"I can work with that," I agree, relief flooding through me. "Though there is one promise I'd like to make, if you'll let me."

"What's that?" she asks, curiosity in her eyes.

"No more disappearing acts," I say solemnly. "Whatever happens between us, good or bad, I promise to face it head-on. No running away, no decisions made unilaterally for 'your own good.'"

A smile blooms on her face, lighting her eyes from within. "I think I can accept that promise," she says. "And make the same one in return."

I reach for her hand, entwining our fingers. "So we're doing this? Whatever 'this' is?"

"We're trying," she clarifies. "With open eyes and open hearts."

"In that case," I say, tugging her gently closer, "would it be alright if I kissed you again? Just to confirm last night wasn't a fluke?"

Annie's laugh is soft, musical. "I think that would be acceptable," she agrees, her eyes dancing with humor and something deeper. "For scientific purposes, of course."

"Of course," I murmur, leaning in to capture her lips with mine.

This kiss is different from last night's—less hesitant, more certain. Annie's arms wind around my neck, careful of my injured shoulder, as she presses closer. My good arm encircles her waist, holding her against me as the kiss deepens, years of longing finding expression in this silent communion.

When we finally part, both slightly breathless, Annie's smile is like sunrise after a long night. "Definitely not a fluke," she confirms.

"Definitely not," I agree, reluctant to release her.

She steps back slightly, though her hands remain on my shoulders. "I should get home," she says, regret in her tone. "The bakery—"

"Is closed on Sundays," I remind her. "Lana told me."

"True," she acknowledges. "But I have festival preparations, contest judging forms to review..."

"Have breakfast with me first," I counter. "I make a mean French toast."

Her resolve visibly weakens. "Well, when you put it that way..."

We work together in the kitchen, moving around each other with growing ease. I slice bread while Annie whisks eggs and cinnamon. She finds berries in the refrigerator while I heat the griddle. Every time we work together like this, in sync with each other, I get the feeling that we've been doing this for years.

Over breakfast, our conversation turns to the upcoming Spring Bloom Festival, particularly the lantern release I'm responsible for overseeing—albeit from a supervisory position given my injury.

"How does it work? Give me the behind-the-scenes scoop," Annie asks.

"There isn't much behind-the-scenes. It's pretty simple," I explain with a shrug. "Each person receives a paper lantern with a small fuel cell. You light it, make a wish or say a prayer, and release it into the night sky. Hundreds of them rising together, floating over the waterfall—it's supposed to be quite a sight, as I am sure you know."

"Yes, it's magical," she says, a touch of wistfulness in her voice.

"And this year is special—it's the seventy-fifth anniversary. The mayor's gone all out with commemorative lanterns featuring the town seal."

"Will you be releasing one?" she asks.

"Tradition says the fire chief always releases the first lantern," I tell her. "Sets the tone for the event."

"What will you wish for?" Her question is light, curious.

I meet her eyes across the table. "If I tell you, it won't come true."

A slight blush colors her cheeks, as if she can guess the nature of my wish. "Fair enough."

After breakfast, I walk Annie to her truck, lingering on the porch steps. The spring morning is beautiful. Birds are singing, flowers are blooming in neighboring yards, and the air's fresh and clean after last night's rain.

"The Spring Ball is Friday night," I remind her. "Are we still on for the opening dance?"

"Absolutely," she confirms.

I lean in, unable to resist stealing one more kiss before she leaves. This one is brief, a promise of more to come. "Drive safely," I murmur against her lips.

"Always," she replies softly.

I watch her drive away, a sense of contentment settling over me that I haven't felt in years. Not the passionate infatuation of youth, or the comfortable familiarity I'd shared with Lisa, but something new—a quiet certainty that despite all odds, Annie Barrett and I have found our way back to each other.

The rest of my day passes in a pleasant haze. Maddie returns from her sleepover full of stories about her friend's family and their plans for the festival. I listen attentively, grateful for her easy acceptance of this new life we're building in Firelight Falls.

"So, what did you do while I was gone? Was someone here?" she asks casually, eyeing the two mugs and the rest of the breakfast dishes drying on the dish rack.

I smile at her directness, a trait she definitely got from me. "Yes, Annie came to ask about my appointment."

"This morning?"

"Last night."

Her eyebrows raise, and she looks pointedly at the breakfast dishes again.

"It's not like that," I say.

Maddie studies me for a moment. "Something's different about you, though," she declares. "You look... I don't know. Happier."

I consider deflecting, but our recent conversations about honesty win out. "Annie and I are figuring things out. Taking it slow, seeing where it leads."

To my surprise, Maddie smiles. "Good," she says simply. "She's good for you, Dad. Makes you less grumpy."

"I'm not grumpy," I protest, feigning offense.

"Since Mom died? Yeah, sometimes you were," she says, catching me off guard. "Not your fault. You were sad, and trying not to show it. But lately... you seem lighter. More like the dad I remember from before."

Children see more than we give them credit for. "Is that okay with you?" I ask. "Annie and I?"

"Yeah," she says finally. "I think Mom would approve. She always said she wanted you to be happy if something happened to her."

The simple statement brings unexpected tears to my eyes. Lisa had indeed said those words in the last months of her illness. I'd dismissed them, unable to imagine future happiness without her. Yet here I am three years later, feeling the first stirrings of new joy, new possibility.

"Thank you for saying that," I tell Maddie, voice rough with emotion. "It means more than you know."

She shrugs, typically teenage in her dismissal of emotional moments. "Just don't get all mushy in public, okay? I still have to live in this town."

I laugh, grateful for her lightening of the mood. "I'll do my best to contain the mushiness."

That night, as I prepare for bed, my phone chimes with a text from Annie.

Annie: Thank you for the breakfast. And everything else. Looking forward to our dance practice tomorrow.

I smile.

Counting the hours. Sleep well.

As I drift toward sleep, I think some flames are extinguished, their purpose served, their time complete. But others—the special ones, the rare ones—can be rekindled from even the faintest ember, burning brighter and stronger for having once been lost.

Annie and I are those embers, I think drowsily. Tenderly being coaxed back to life.

# Annie

THE SPRING BLOOM FESTIVAL begins tomorrow, and Firelight Falls vibrates with anticipation. Main Street has been transformed with blooming flower baskets hanging from every lamppost, vendor booths lining the sidewalks, and colorful banners spanning the thoroughfare. The waterfall park is adorned with twinkling lights and lantern stations, ready for the last event.

At the bakery, we've been working overtime to prepare everything. Display cases overflow with festival-themed treats—flower-shaped cookies, bluebonnet cupcakes, and special edition Spring Bloom pies featuring local fruits in a decorative lattice pattern that took hours to perfect.

"Annie, the judges' packets for the baking contest are ready," Lana announces, setting a stack of folders on the counter. "Name tags, scoring sheets, and tasting notes are all organized and color-coded."

"You're amazing," I tell her gratefully. "I don't know how I'd manage all this without you."

"You'd manage," she assures me. "Just with more panic and less sleep."

I laugh and shrug my shoulders. "Fair enough."

The bell above the door chimes, and I look up to see Maddie Colton entering the bakery. She's alone, backpack slung over one shoulder, her dark hair pulled into a messy bun. She spots me and waves, making her way through the afternoon crowd to the counter.

"Hi, Annie," she says, her smile reminiscent of her father's. "Wow, it's packed in here."

"Festival fever," I explain. "Everyone wants treats for the opening parade tomorrow. What can I get you?"

"Actually," she begins, looking suddenly uncertain, "I was wondering if you had time to talk? About something... personal?"

Her hesitant request catches me by surprise. Though Maddie and I have developed a friendly rapport over the past weeks, we've never had a private conversation without Jake present.

"Of course," I say, trying to hide my curiosity. "Let me take a quick break. Lana, can you handle things for fifteen minutes?"

Lana nods, giving Maddie a warm smile. "Take your time. I've got this covered."

I lead Maddie through the kitchen to the small office in the back, where we can speak privately. It's cluttered with baking books, order forms, and festival preparation materials, but I clear a space for her to sit across from my desk.

"Can I get you anything?" I offer. "Water? Hot chocolate?"

"I'm good," she says, though her nervous fidgeting suggests otherwise. "Thanks."

I settle into my chair, giving her my full attention. "What's on your mind?"

Maddie takes a deep breath, as if gathering courage. "It's about the Spring Ball tomorrow night," she begins. "Dad mentioned you two are doing the opening dance."

"That's right," I say, wondering where this is heading. "It's tradition for the fire chief and the baking contest coordinator."

She nods, twisting a bracelet around her wrist. "And after that... are you, like, his date for the rest of the night?"

"We haven't really discussed details," I tell her honestly. "But I suppose we would spend the evening together, yes. Is that okay with you?"

Maddie looks down at her hands, clearly hesitant about something. "Yes, it's fine. It's not that. It's just... Dad's been so busy with the festival planning and his shoulder injury and... well, everything. I don't think he remembered I need a dress for tomorrow."

"Have you mentioned it to him?" I ask gently.

She shakes her head. "I didn't want to add to his stress. I don't even know if I'd be going or not. It's not like I have anyone to go with, anyway. I barely know anyone here."

The vulnerability beneath her casual tone touches my heart. Fifteen's such a hard age. You're no longer a child, not quite an adult, and navigating new emotions and experiences while trying to appear unfazed by it all. It also becomes clear now why she wanted to know if Jake and I would spend the evening together.

"Well, of course, you are going to the Ball. The Spring Ball isn't just for couples," I tell her. "Lots of people go in groups, or with family members. It's a community celebration. You'll be right there with your father and me."

"I guess," she says, a look of relief taking over her countenance.

A thought occurs to me, and I hope I'm not overstepping. "Would you like to go shopping? For a dress, I mean. I could use a break from festival preparations, and I know all the best shops in town."

Her face brightens immediately. "Really? You wouldn't mind?"

"I'd love to," I assure her, checking my watch. "The boutique on Elm Street is open until six. If we left now, we'd have plenty of time."

"But what about the bakery?" she asks, glancing toward the busy front.

"Lana and Marjorie can handle closing," I say. "Let me grab my purse and let them know."

Minutes later, we're walking down Main Street toward Primrose Boutique, Firelight Falls' premier clothing store. The spring afternoon is perfect. Warm sunshine warms my face, a gentle breeze keeps it from being too hot, and the scent of jasmine and honeysuckle perfumes the air.

"So," I begin casually, "how are you liking Firelight Falls so far? It must be quite a change from Houston."

Maddie considers the question thoughtfully. "It's different," she acknowledges. "Smaller. Quieter. But nice in its own way. People actually know each other here."

"That's both the charm and the challenge of small-town living," I observe. "Everyone knows your business, but they also have your back when it matters."

"I'm seeing that," she says. "After Dad got hurt in the fire, so many people dropped off food and offered to help. We hardly knew any of them."

"That's Firelight Falls," I tell her with a smile. "We take care of our own."

We reach Primrose Boutique, a charming storefront with elegant window displays filled with spring fashions. Inside the shop is a treasure trove of clothing, accessories, and formal wear.

"Annie!" Eleanor Primrose, the owner, greets me warmly. "What a lovely surprise."

"Hello, Eleanor," I say. "We're on a mission to find a Spring Ball dress for Maddie here. Chief Colton's daughter."

Eleanor's eyes light up. "Of course! I've been hoping you'd visit, dear," she tells Maddie. "We have a beautiful selection of dresses perfect for tomorrow night."

For the next hour, we lose ourselves in the delight of dress shopping. Maddie tries on a parade of options—a sunny yellow sundress, a sophisticated navy blue A-line, a romantic pink confection with layers of tulle. Each time she emerges from the dressing room, her confidence visibly grows as both Eleanor and I offer genuine compliments.

"What about this one?" Eleanor suggests, presenting a dress in soft sea foam green with delicate silver embroidery along the bodice. "It would complement her coloring beautifully."

Maddie disappears into the dressing room. When she comes back out, we both gasp softly. The dress is perfect. It's age-appropriate yet sophisticated, highlighting her slender frame while the color brings out the blue of her eyes and the warm undertones in her dark hair.

"Maddie..." I breathe. "You look absolutely beautiful."

She turns toward the full-length mirror, uncertainty giving way to wonder as she takes in her reflection. "It's perfect," she whispers, running her hands over the silky fabric.

"Your father will be speechless," Eleanor declares. "Every young man at the ball will ask for a dance."

Maddie blushes. "Do you really think so?"

"Absolutely. You'll be the belle of the ball."

While Maddie changes back into her regular clothes, Eleanor shows me the price tag. The dress is lovely but expensive. More than a teenager's budget would typically allow.

"I'd like to pay for it," I tell Eleanor quietly. "But let's tell her it's on sale."

Eleanor nods, understanding immediately. "I'll wrap it up beautifully."

When Maddie emerges, I've already handed over my credit card. "Good news," I tell her. "Eleanor is having a special festival discount today. The dress is thirty percent off."

"Really?" Maddie looks between us, not entirely convinced but clearly wanting to believe it.

"Festival special," Eleanor confirms smoothly. "And I'll throw in a matching wrap at no extra charge."

As we leave the boutique with the carefully wrapped dress box, Maddie turns to me. "Thank you," she says. "Not just for helping with the dress, but for... making me feel welcome. Like I belong here."

"You belong here, Maddie. And I'm happy to help, truly."

We walk in comfortable silence for a few moments before she speaks again. "Can I ask you something personal?"

"Of course," I reply, curious about what's on her mind.

"Did you love my dad? Back when you were young, I mean."

The directness of her question catches me by surprise, though I suppose I should have expected it. Jake's daughter is perceptive and straightforward, much like her father.

"Yes," I answer honestly. "Very much."

She nods, as if this confirms something she already suspected. "And now? Do you love him now?"

I hesitate. "Your father and I are rediscovering each other," I tell her carefully. "We've both changed a lot in twenty years. But I care about him a lot."

"He cares about you too," she says matter-of-factly. "I can tell. He smiles more when you're around, or even when someone just mentions your name."

I can't help but smile. "That's good to know."

"My mom would've liked you," Maddie continues, her tone light despite the weight of her words. "She always said Dad needed someone who could match his intensity, challenge him when he needed it."

"She sounds like a remarkable woman," I say sincerely. "Your dad speaks of her with such respect and love."

"She was the best," Maddie agrees, a wistful smile touching her lips. "Funny, and creative, and super smart. She never talked down to me, even when I was little. She always treated me like my thoughts mattered."

"That's a wonderful gift to give a child," I say.

Maddie nods, her expression thoughtful. "When she got sick, everything changed. Dad tried so hard to keep things normal, but we both knew it wouldn't be."

The pain in her voice is palpable. I resist the urge to offer platitudes, sensing she needs simply to be heard.

"The hardest part wasn't even losing her," Maddie continues, her voice dropping. "It was watching Dad try to be both parents afterward. He was so determined to do everything right, to not let me see how much he was hurting. But I could tell."

"Of course, you could," I say. "Children often understand more than adults realize."

She glances at me, a flash of relief in her eyes. "Exactly. And then we moved here, and everything changed again. New school, new house, new town. But also... a different Dad. More like how I remember him before Mom got sick."

"Firelight Falls has been good for him," I say.

"It's not just the town," Maddie says. "It's you. Whatever was between you guys before, it helped him remember who he used to be. Before all the sad stuff."

I'm speechless. How do I respond to that?

"Thank you for telling me that," I say finally. "And for being so open about your mom. I know that can't be easy."

Maddie shrugs, though the droop in her shoulders suggests its harder for her than she lets on. "Dad says it's important to talk about her, to keep her memory alive. And he's right. I don't want to forget anything about her."

"You never will," I assure her. "She'll always be a part of you."

"Want to come in?" I offer when we reach the bakery. "I can pack up some treats for you to take home."

"Actually," Maddie says, glancing at her phone, "Dad's waiting for me at home. We're supposed to have dinner with Aunt Caroline tonight."

"Okay," I say, hiding my disappointment at not seeing Jake this evening. "Will you tell him about the dress?"

She grins mischievously. "Nope. I want it to be a surprise tomorrow night. Can you keep a secret?"

"Absolutely," I promise. "Your dad won't hear a word from me." I mime zipping my lips, and she giggles.

"Thanks, Annie," she says, her voice suddenly soft. "For everything."

On impulse, I give her a quick hug, relieved when she returns it. "I'll see you tomorrow at the festival," I say. "Your dad and I have to be at the opening ceremony at ten."

"I'll be there."

I watch her walk away, the dress box carefully cradled in her arms. Despite losing her mom so young, she's truly growing into a remarkable young woman. A credit to her parents' love.

Inside the bakery, Lana is supervising the final customers of the day. She raises a questioning eyebrow as I return.

"Shopping trip was a success," I report. "Maddie found the perfect dress for tomorrow night."

"Good," Lana says. "And how was spending time with your potential future stepdaughter?"

I nearly choke at her phrasing. "Lana! We are nowhere near that stage."

"Yet," she adds with a grin. "But you have to admit, things are progressing nicely between you and Chief Hottie."

I can't deny the claim, even if it is embarrassing to be discussing this right now. In the weeks since Jake's return to Firelight Falls, we've moved from awkward reunion to tentative friendship to something deeper. "We're taking it slow," I remind her. "One day at a time."

"Mmm-hmm," Lana hums skeptically. "That's why you glow like a teenager every time he walks in here."

Before I can plan a suitable retort, my phone chimes with a text message.

> Jake: Just heard you took Maddie shopping. Thank you. I completely dropped the ball on the Spring Ball dress situation.

I smile.

> My pleasure. She's a wonderful young woman. You should be very proud.

I don't wait long before my phone dings with another text.

> Jake: I am. Of her, and increasingly of myself for having the good sense to fall for a woman who treats my daughter so kindly.

My heart flutters.

> She makes it easy. She has her father's charm.

> Jake: And her mother's insight. Whatever she said to you today, I hope it wasn't too overwhelming. She speaks her mind.

I consider how to respond, not wanting to betray Maddie's trust.

> It was lovely, actually. We had a good talk. You've raised an amazing daughter, Jake.

> Jake: We did our best.

The love he had for Lisa could sting, but it doesn't.

> Jake: See you tomorrow at the festival?

> Bright and early. Try to get some rest tonight. Big day ahead.

> Jake: You too. Sweet dreams, Annie. x

That small "x" at the end of his message sends a flutter through my stomach that feels remarkably like the ones I experienced at seventeen, when Jake Colton first began signing his notes to me with that same symbol.

Some things, it seems, never change.

· · · · • · • · · ·

The next morning dawns clear and perfect—as if the weather itself is celebrating the Spring Bloom Festival. I arrive at the bakery at five, working alongside Lana and Marjorie to prepare for what will undoubtedly be our busiest day of the year.

By nine-thirty, with the bakery humming smoothly under Lana's capable supervision, I change into my festival outfit—a cornflower blue sundress , paired with comfortable white sandals that will allow me to navigate the long day ahead.

The town square is already buzzing with activity when I arrive. Vendor booths line the perimeter, offering everything from handcrafted jewelry to local honey. The bandstand is draped in floral garlands, ready for the community orchestra's afternoon performance. Children dart between exhibits, faces painted with butterflies and flowers, while parents chat in clusters, greeting neighbors and visitors alike.

I spot Jake immediately, standing near the ceremonial stage where Mayor Wilson will officially open the festival. He's in his dress uniform—navy blue with brass buttons, badge gleaming in the morning sun. His left arm is out of the sling but held carefully, a reminder of his still-healing injury.

He sees me approaching and smiles, the warmth in his eyes sending a pleasant shiver down my spine. "Good morning," he says, his voice rough. "You look beautiful."

"Thank you," I say. "You clean up pretty well yourself, Chief Colton."

His smile widens at my teasing tone. "The uniform does most of the work," he says. "How's the bakery booth coming along?"

"Lana has it under control. Have you seen Maddie yet?"

"She's helping Caroline set up the information booth," he says, gesturing across the square. "Turns out my daughter has a hidden talent for organization."

"Not so hidden," I say, remembering our conversation about her yearbook committee work. "She's quite impressive."

Jake's expression softens with paternal pride. "She is, isn't she? I got lucky in the daughter department."

"She feels the same way about her dad," I tell him.

Before Jake can respond, Mayor Wilson approaches, looking handsome in a seersucker suit with a carnation boutonniere. "Annie! Chief Colton! Perfect timing. We're about to begin the opening ceremony."

The next hour passes in a whirlwind of official duties—Mayor Wilson's welcoming speech, the ceremonial cutting of a ribbon adorned with spring flowers, my introduction of the baking contest judges. Jake presents the festival safety protocols, and then the festival shifts into full swing.

Jake and I find a quiet moment at the edge of the square to people watch.

"One duty down, several to go," he says, glancing around at the crowd. "The Spring Ball is tonight, then the lantern release tomorrow evening."

"And the baking contest judging this afternoon," I add. "I should check the competition area soon."

Jake glances at his watch. "I have to inspect the lantern stations at the waterfall park. Walk with me?"

"I'd like that," I say, falling into step beside him.

As we navigate through the festival crowds, I can feel the glances and smiles directed our way. In a town the size of Firelight Falls, our developing relationship is undoubtedly a topic of interest.

"People are watching us," I murmur, leaning closer to Jake.

"Let them," he replies with a grin. "Gives them something to talk about besides cattle prices and weather forecasts."

I laugh, appreciating his perspective. "I suppose we are more interesting than rainfall predictions."

At the waterfall park, festival workers are arranging lantern distribution stations and safety barriers for tomorrow night's release. Jake moves among them with natural authority, checking placements, confirming procedures, ensuring every detail is addressed.

I watch him work, struck by the contrast between the Jake I knew at twenty-two and the man before me now. The reckless energy of his youth has been channeled into purposeful leadership, his natural charisma tempered with wisdom and experience.

"Everything looks good," he says finally, returning to my side. "Williams has the firefighter assignments under control. Barring any emergencies, tomorrow night should go smoothly."

"Let's hope for no emergencies," I say, shaking my head. "You've had more than your share recently."

Jake's hand finds mine, weaving our fingers together. "I don't know about that," he says thoughtfully. "Some emergencies have unexpected silver linings."

"Like dislocated shoulders?" I ask skeptically.

"Like reconnecting with you," he clarifies, his eyes holding mine. "If I hadn't run into that burning building, you might not have stayed over , or given me another chance."

The earnestness in his voice touches me deeply. "I think we were headed there anyway," I tell him softly. "Fire or no fire."

His smile is gentle, hopeful. "You think so?"

"I do," I whisper. "Some things are just... inevitable."

The admission feels both frightening and liberating.

Jake lifts our joined hands, pressing a kiss to my knuckles. "In that case, I'm looking forward to whatever comes next."

"Starting with the Spring Ball tonight," I remind him. "Are you ready for our dance debut?"

"As ready as I'll ever be," he says with mock solemnity. "Though I'll admit to some nerves. Half the town will be watching."

"Just follow my lead," I say, tossing a wink in his direction. "I'll make you look good."

His laugh is warm. "You always did."

· · · ● · ● · · ·

The afternoon passes in a blur of activity. The baking contest draws a record number of entries, keeping the judges and me occupied for hours. Lana reports record sales at the bakery booth, and Marjorie has already made three supply runs back to the shop.

By the time the contest winners are announced—Mrs. Henderson's strawberry-rhubarb pie taking the coveted Best in Show ribbon—the afternoon sun is fading. I check my watch, realizing I have barely two hours to prepare for the Spring Ball.

"Annie!" Caroline's voice cuts through the crowd. She approaches with Maddie beside her, both looking flushed and happy from the day's festivities. "Fantastic contest! Mom would have loved seeing all those pies lined up for judging."

"It was a success," I agree, smiling at them both. "Have you two been enjoying the festival?"

"It's amazing," Maddie says, a huge grin plastered on her face. "So much bigger than I expected. We heard the orchestra, tried like five different food booths, and Aunt Caroline won a stuffed bear at the ring toss."

"Beginner's luck," Caroline says, though she clutches the small blue teddy proudly. "We're heading home to get ready for tonight. Need a ride? You look like you could use a break before the ball."

The offer is tempting. My feet ache from hours of standing, and the thought of walking back to the bakery is less than appealing. "That would be wonderful, actually."

In Caroline's car, Maddie chatters excitedly about the festival highlights. I listen with genuine interest, touched by how quickly she's embraced Firelight Falls and its traditions.

As we near the bakery, she asks, "Are you nervous about the dance?"

"A little," I admit. "But we've practiced, so I think we'll manage without embarrassing ourselves too badly."

"You'll be great," Maddie says. "Dad's been practicing when he thinks no one's watching. I caught him counting steps in the kitchen yesterday."

The image of Jake rehearsing dance steps alone makes me smile. "That's dedication."

"He wants to impress you," she says, as if stating an obvious fact.

Caroline catches my eye in the rearview mirror, her expression amused. "Out of the mouths of babes," she murmurs.

At the bakery, I thank them for the ride and promise to see them at the ball. Upstairs in my apartment, I indulge in a long, hot shower, washing away the festival dust and soothing my tired muscles. As I prepare for the evening, applying makeup and styling my hair into loose waves, I hum the waltz Jake and I practiced—our song, in a way.

My dress for the ball is a deep emerald green that brings out my eyes, with a flowing skirt perfect for dancing. As I slip it on, adjusting the delicate straps, I can't help but wonder what Jake will think. Will he remember that green was always his favorite color on me?

A light knock at my apartment door interrupts my thoughts. When I open the door, however, it's not Jake who stands there, but Maddie. She's stunning in her sea-foam dress, hair arranged in an elegant updo with tendrils framing her face, a touch of subtle makeup enhancing her natural beauty.

"Maddie," I say, genuinely stunned by her appearance, "you look absolutely gorgeous."

She smiles shyly. "So do you. That color is amazing on you."

"Thank you," I say, gesturing her inside. "Is your dad with you?"

"No, Aunt Caroline brought me here. Dad had to oversee something at the Ball," she explains. "I wanted to ask... would you help me with something?"

"Of course," I say, curious. "What do you need?"

From her small purse, Maddie produces a delicate silver necklace with a pearl pendant. "This was my mom's," she says quietly. "Dad gave it to me before we left tonight. Said she'd want me to have it for my first Spring Ball. But I can't get the clasp to work by myself."

The significance of this moment—Maddie asking me to help her with her mother's necklace, when she could have easily asked Caroline—feels monumental. It's a gesture of trust and acceptance that goes beyond our shopping trip or casual conversations.

"I'd be honored," I tell her, taking the necklace reverently.

She turns, lifting her hair to expose her neck. I carefully secure the delicate chain, adjusting the pearl to lie perfectly at the hollow of her throat.

"There," I say, my voice slightly unsteady. "Perfect."

Maddie turns back to face me, her fingers touching the pearl. "Mom wore this the night Dad asked her to marry him," she tells me.

"She would be so proud of you," I say.

Maddie's eyes shine with unshed tears. "Dad says the same thing."

"Your dad is a wise man," I tell her. "When he's not running into burning buildings, that is."

She laughs, the emotional moment lightening. "True. Speaking of Dad, we should probably get going. He's probably waiting for us at the Ball."

"Let me grab my wrap and purse," I say, gathering my things. "Caroline's driving us?"

"She's waiting downstairs," Maddie confirms. "Said to tell you she's not a taxi service, but she'll make an exception for tonight."

I smile, recognizing Caroline's characteristic blend of sarcasm and generosity. "Then we shouldn't keep her waiting."

As we leave the apartment, Maddie pauses at the door. "Thank you," she says. "I'm glad we met."

In that moment, I realize how much this young woman means to me, not because she's Jake's daughter, but because of who she is in her own right.

"Thank you, Maddie," I reply softly. "For letting me be a part of your life."

Her smile—so like her father's—warms me from within. Together, we descend the stairs to where Caroline waits, ready to usher us toward an evening of dancing, community celebration, and the quiet kindling of hope for a future none of us could have expected just months ago.

# Jake

THE SPRING BALL TRANSFORMS the Firelight Falls Community Center from a generic municipal building into a magical wonderland. The planning committee has outdone itself. Twinkling lights cascade from the ceiling, floral arrangements burst from every corner, and a canopy of pastel streamers creates the illusion of a spring sky overhead. The community orchestra occupies a small stage at one end of the room, their formal attire adding to the evening's elegance.

I adjust the collar of my dress uniform for the tenth time, scanning the growing crowd for any sign of Annie or Maddie. Caroline just arrived, but cryptically reported that "the ladies are making an entrance" when I asked about their whereabouts.

"Nervous?" Ben Martinez appears beside me, looking sharp in a dark suit.

"About the dance? A little," I admit. "Annie's been coaching me, but I'm not exactly Fred Astaire."

Ben chuckles. "I'm sure you'll do fine. Though I have to say, Chief, you're a lucky man. Annie Barrett is quite a woman."

There's something in his tone that catches my attention. "She is," I agree, studying him more carefully. "Have you known her long?"

"Five years," he says casually. "Since I moved to town. Always thought she was special, but the timing never worked out."

The admission that Ben had been interested in Annie stirs an unexpected flare of possessiveness in my chest. I tamp it down, reminding myself that Annie has built a life here during my absence, formed connections and relationships that have nothing to do with me.

"Well," I say, offering my hand, "I appreciate you looking out for her while I was being an idiot elsewhere in the state."

Ben laughs, accepting the handshake. "Can't argue with that assessment. But for what it's worth, I think she's happier now than I've seen her in years. Whatever you're doing, keep it up."

Before I can respond, the crowd near the entrance shifts, and conversation momentarily falters. I turn to see what has captured everyone's attention, and my breath catches in my throat.

Annie stands in the doorway, radiant in a gown the color of deep forest moss. The fabric flows around her like water, catching the light as she moves. Her hair falls in soft waves around her shoulders, and a simple silver pendant nestles at her collarbone. She's beautiful in a way that outshines everyone else in the room.

Beside her stands Maddie, nearly unrecognizable in a shimmering sea-foam dress that transforms her from a teenager to a young woman before my eyes. The pearl necklace that once belonged to her mother gleams at her throat, a perfect complement to her dark hair and fair skin.

"Wow," Ben murmurs beside me. "They certainly know how to steal the spotlight."

I barely hear him, already moving toward the doorway, drawn by an invisible thread that has connected me to Annie Barrett since we were children. When she spots me approaching, her smile blooms like a flower opening to the sun, warm and genuine and just for me.

"You look..." I begin, words failing as I reach her side.

"So do you," she says, understanding perfectly. Her eyes take in my dress uniform, appreciation in her gaze. "Very dashing, Chief Colton."

"Dad!" Maddie steps forward, a hint of uncertainty beneath her excitement. "What do you think?"

Emotion tightens my throat. "You're beautiful, sweetheart," I tell her, voice rough with feeling. "Absolutely beautiful. Your mother's necklace is perfect."

She touches the pearl, smiling softly. "Annie helped me put it on."

The image of Annie helping my daughter with Lisa's necklace flashes through my mind, making my heart swell. Before I can respond, Mayor Wilson approaches in his tuxedo. "Ah, there you are! The opening dance begins in five minutes. Are you two ready?"

Annie's hand slips into mine, warm and reassuring. "As we'll ever be," she answers for us both.

"Excellent!" The mayor beams. "Maddie, your aunt is saving you a seat near the front. Best view in the house!"

As the mayor bustles away, I turn to my daughter. "Will you be okay while we do this dance thing?"

She rolls her eyes, every bit a moody teenager despite the elegant attire. "Dad, I'm fifteen, not five. Go be an honorary Spring Bloom Festival person. I'll be fine."

Annie laughs at her phrasing. "Honorary Spring Bloom Festival person," she repeats. "I like that. Much less intimidating than 'opening dance performers.'"

With a final reassuring smile for Maddie, I escort Annie toward the dance floor, which has been cleared in the center of the room. The orchestra conductor catches our eye, nodding to show they're ready when we are.

"Any last-minute advice?" I murmur to Annie as we take our positions.

"Just follow my lead," she says, her eyes dancing with humor. "And try not to step on my toes. This dress cost a fortune."

"No pressure," I say, suddenly much calmer with her familiar teasing.

Mayor Wilson steps forward to address the assembled crowd. "Ladies and gentlemen, welcome to the seventy-fifth annual Spring Bloom Ball! As tradition dictates, we begin with the opening dance, performed this year by our Fire Chief, Jake Colton, and our Baking Contest Coordinator, Annie Barrett."

Applause ripples through the room as the mayor steps back. The orchestra strikes up the familiar waltz—the same one Annie and I practiced in her apartment.

As I take Annie in my arms, right hand at her waist, left carefully positioned despite my healing shoulder, everything else fades away.

We move, finding our rhythm immediately. One-two-three, one-two-three, around the floor in perfect synchrony. Annie follows my lead effortlessly, though we both know she could just as easily lead me. It's a partnership, a balance, each supporting the other through the turns and steps.

"Everyone's watching," Annie whispers, though she doesn't seem concerned.

"Let them," I reply, echoing my earlier sentiment. "We're giving them something worth seeing."

Her smile widens at my confidence, and I spin her in a careful turn that sends her skirt flaring elegantly around her ankles. When she returns to my arms, her eyes hold a spark of surprised delight.

"You've been practicing," she accuses lightly.

"Maybe a little," I acknowledge. "Maddie caught me counting steps in the kitchen yesterday."

Annie laughs, the sound blending perfectly with the music. "Dedication."

"Motivation," I murmur, drawing her slightly closer. "I wanted to make you proud."

Her expression softens. "You already do, Jake. In ways that have nothing to do with dancing."

We continue our circuit of the dance floor, moving together as the music swells around us. Other couples have joined now, but I see only Annie. There's a sparkle in her eyes, and a flush on her cheeks. She fits perfectly in my arms as if designed to be there.

As the music draws to a close, I execute one final turn, dipping Annie slightly in a move we hadn't practiced but feels right. She follows my lead without hesitation, trusting me to keep her safe.

When we straighten, the room erupts in applause. Annie's eyes meet mine, bright with exhilaration and a feeling we aren't ready to name yet.

"Not bad, Chief Colton," she murmurs as we bow to the crowd. "Not bad at all."

"I had an excellent teacher," I say, leading her from the dance floor. We make our way to where Maddie sits with Caroline, both watching us with looks of approval.

"Dad, that was amazing!" Maddie exclaims. "You didn't step on her feet once!"

"Your father is full of surprises," Annie tells her with a warm smile.

"Speaking of surprises," Caroline interjects, "Maddie, isn't that Ryan Mitchell heading this way? From your history class?"

Maddie whips around, her expression a mix of alarm and excitement. Sure enough, a tall, sandy-haired boy approaches our table, looking nervous but determined in a slightly large suit.

"Hi, Maddie," he says, his voice cracking slightly. "You look really nice. I was wondering if maybe... you might want to dance? With me?"

The hope in his expression is painfully familiar. It's the same look I wore when asking Annie to our first school dance nearly twenty-five years ago. I feel a sudden surge of protectiveness, coupled with the realization that my daughter is growing up faster than I can comprehend.

Maddie glances at me, a silent question in her eyes. I nod slightly, giving her permission, though she doesn't really need it.

"I'd like that," she tells Ryan, standing gracefully. "Dad, Annie, I'll be back in a little while."

I watch as the young man leads my daughter onto the dance floor, their movements awkward as they find their footing together.

"She'll be fine," Annie assures me, reading my thoughts. "He seems like a nice boy."

"They all seem nice until they break your daughter's heart," I grumble, though there's no real heat in it.

Caroline laughs. "And you would know nothing about breaking hearts, would you, little brother?"

Annie intervenes before I can respond. "I think I need something to drink after all that dancing. Care to escort me to the punch bowl, Chief Colton?"

Grateful for the diversion, I offer my arm. "It would be my pleasure, Ms. Barrett."

As we make our way across the room, stopping frequently to greet people and accept compliments on our dance, I'm struck by how naturally Annie moves in these circles. Everyone knows her, respects her, and values her contribution to the community. In the weeks since my return, I've begun to understand just how integral she is to Firelight Falls—not just as the bakery owner, but as a friend, mentor, and touchstone for so many.

"You're thinking awfully hard over there," Annie says as we reach the refreshment table. "Everything okay?"

"Just realizing how much everyone loves you," I tell her honestly. "How important you are to this town."

A slight blush colors her cheeks. "Firelight Falls has been good to me," she says, shrugging her shoulders. "I try to return the favor."

I hand her a cup of punch, our fingers brushing in the exchange. "Dance with me again?" I ask. "I want to hold you close a little longer."

"I'd like that very much."

This dance is less of a performance, and more about connection. Annie rests her head against my shoulder as we sway to a slower melody, her body fitted perfectly against mine. Around us, other couples move in similar embrace, but we might as well be alone for all the attention I pay them.

"I was afraid I'd forgotten how to do this," I confess quietly. "Not just the dancing, but... this. Being with someone. Caring for someone beyond Maddie."

Annie lifts her head slightly to meet my eyes. "And have you forgotten?"

"No," I say. "It's different—I'm different—but I haven't forgotten what it's like to want to build a future with someone."

Her eyes search mine, looking for the truth behind the words. "Are we building a future, Jake?"

"I hope so," I tell her. "I'd like to try if you're willing."

"I'm willing," she says. "Scared, but willing."

"Scared is okay," I say. "Scared means it matters."

She nods, settling back against my shoulder as we continue to move with the music. "It matters," she affirms. "More than I expected it to, if I'm being honest."

"For me too," I admit. "Coming back to Firelight Falls, I hoped to see you, to explain, and maybe to earn forgiveness. I never dared hope for a second chance."

"Life is full of surprises," Annie murmurs against my uniform jacket. "Some tragic, some wonderful. The trick is recognizing the wonderful ones when they appear."

"And is this," I ask, tightening my arm around her waist, "a wonderful surprise?"

She lifts her face to mine, eyes reflecting the twinkling lights overhead. "The most wonderful," she whispers.

The honesty in her expression, the quiet certainty in her voice, fills me with a hope so intense it borders on pain. Twenty years ago, I left this woman behind, convinced I was protecting her from the chaos of my life. Now, against all odds, she's giving me a chance to prove I've learned from that mistake, to show her that some loves are worth fighting for, worth staying for, worth building a future around.

Across the room, I glimpse Maddie, still dancing with the sandy-haired boy. She sees me watching and offers a small smile and thumbs-up over her partner's shoulder. My daughter, approving of the woman in my arms. My past and present coming together in ways I never imagined.

"Jake?" Annie's voice pulls me back to her. "Where did you go just now?"

"Nowhere," I assure her, tightening my arms around her. "I'm right here. Where I belong."

And as the music continues and Annie nestles closer in my embrace, I know with absolute certainty that it's true. After years of wandering, of building a life elsewhere, of loss and grief and healing, I've come home. Not just to Firelight Falls, but to Annie Barrett, to the love we once shared.

Hope kindles within me, a steady flame that warms me from the inside out. And this time, I vow silently, I won't let it go out.

# Annie

THE LAST DAY OF the Spring Bloom Festival dawns warm and clear, a perfect Texas spring morning. I wake with the lingering sensation of Jake's arms around me from our dances the night before.

The memory brings a smile to my face as I stretch lazily. The Spring Ball had been magical. Our opening dance was flawless. But it's the quiet moments with Jake as we swayed together under twinkling lights that mean the most. His words replay in my mind. "I'm right here. Where I belong."

A commitment, a promise, a declaration all in one.

My phone chimes with a text message.

> **Jake:** Looking forward to seeing you at the lantern release tonight. Coffee first?

His thoughtfulness makes me smile so big my cheeks hurt.

> Good morning! Coffee sounds perfect. The bakery at 9?

I glance at the clock. Plenty of time to do something with my hair.

> Jake: I'll be there. Maddie says to tell you she's still dreaming about that dress. Think you created a shopping monster.

I laugh, picturing Maddie's delight in her Spring Ball finery.

> Guilty as charged. She looked beautiful.

> Jake: Like her shopping companion. ;)

Setting my phone aside, I force myself to get out of bed and get ready for the day ahead. The festival's finale is tonight, and as a committee member, I have responsibilities to fulfill before then. But first, coffee with Jake.

The bakery is closed for business on festival Sunday, but the kitchen stays open for special orders. When I arrive downstairs, Lana is already there, decorating cupcakes for a post-festival baby shower.

"Someone's glowing this morning," she says without looking up from her piping. "Good night at the ball, Cinderella?"

"Very," I say, unable to contain my smile. "The dance went beautifully."

"I heard," she says, finally meeting my eyes. "Mrs. Henderson said you two looked, and I quote, 'like you were dancing on clouds.' High praise from our town's most discerning critic."

I feel a blush warming my cheeks. "It was nice," I admit. "Really nice."

"Mmm-hmm." Lana's knowing look suggests she understands exactly how 'nice' it was. "Things seem to be progressing rapidly for someone who was determined to maintain a professional distance a few weeks ago."

"Life happens," I say with a shrug, though her observation is fair. My relationship with Jake has grown with startling speed since his return to Firelight Falls.

"Just be careful," Lana says, her tone gentle. "I'm happy for you—truly. But you've worked so hard to build this life... I don't want to see you hurt again."

"I know," I assure her. "We're taking it slow. We've both changed a lot in twenty years."

"Good," she says, returning to her cupcakes. "Because your fire chief just pulled up outside."

My pulse quickens. I move to the mirror behind the counter, checking my appearance. I look casual but put-together in my soft yellow sundress.

The back door opens, and Jake steps in, looking refreshed despite what must have been a late night. He's casual today in jeans and a light blue button-down that brings out his eyes.

"Good morning, ladies," he greets us both, though his gaze lingers on me.

"Morning, Chief," Lana responds. "Don't mind me, just working on these cupcakes. Pretend I'm not here."

Jake smiles at her teasing tone. "Impossible, Lana. Your cupcakes are too extraordinary to ignore."

"Flattery will get you everywhere," she quips.

"The usual?" I ask Jake as I move to the coffee counter.

"Please," he says, leaning against the counter as I prepare two cups—his black with two sugars, mine with a splash of cream.

As I hand Jake his mug, our fingers brush, sending that now-familiar tingle up my arm.

"So," I say, gesturing to a small table in the corner of the kitchen, away from Lana's workstation. "Ready for the grand finale tonight?"

"As ready as we can be," he replies, settling into a chair. "Williams has the firefighter assignments coordinated, safety barriers are in place, and the weather forecast is perfect."

"Sounds like you've thought of everything," I observe.

"Let's hope so," he says. "First major event under my watch as chief. I want it to go smoothly."

"It will," I assure him. "Firelight Falls has been doing the lantern release for decades without incident."

"True," he says. "Though this year is special. Because of the anniversary, Mayor Wilson is expecting record attendance."

We chat easily about festival logistics, community gossip, and Maddie's apparent dance floor success with the sandy-haired boy from her history class.

"Ryan seems like a nice kid," he admits reluctantly. "His father runs the hardware store on Main Street. Good family."

"And Maddie has a good head on her shoulders," I remind him. "You've raised her well."

His expression softens at the compliment. "Lisa deserves most of the credit there," he says. "She was an amazing mother."

The easy way he speaks of his late wife speaks to the love they shared. There's no awkwardness or jealousy in hearing about Lisa. She is part of Jake's story, part of what shaped him into the man sitting across from me now.

"She must have been remarkable," I say sincerely. "Maddie's a wonderful young woman."

Jake reaches across the table, taking my hand in his. "Thank you," he says. "You're so good with her."

The warmth in his eyes sends a flutter through my stomach. Before I can respond, the back door opens again, and Caroline strides in, impeccably dressed as usual.

"There you are," she says to Jake. "I've been calling your cell for the past twenty minutes."

Jake frowns, pulling his phone from his pocket. "The battery died. Sorry. What's up?"

"Mom's having a rough morning," Caroline says, her expression tight with concern. "The nursing staff called. She's agitated, asking for you specifically."

Jake stands immediately, all traces of relaxation vanishing. "I'll head over now. Is she—"

"Physically fine," Caroline assures him. "Just confused, emotional. These episodes seem to be increasing lately."

"I'm sorry about the coffee," Jake says, turning to me. "I need to—"

"Go," I interrupt, squeezing his hand. "Your mother needs you. We'll catch up later."

Relief and gratitude flash across his face. "Thank you for understanding," he says. "I'll call you when things settle down."

After they leave, Lana glances up from her cupcakes. "Everything okay?"

"His mother," I say. "She has dementia, good days and bad. Apparently, today is bad."

Lana nods sympathetically. "That's tough. My grandmother went through something similar before she passed."

"Jake's been so worried about her," I say, gathering our coffee mugs. "It's part of the reason he moved back to Firelight Falls."

"Along with other attractions," Lana observes with a smile. "Speaking of which, what are you wearing to the lantern release tonight? Something fireproof, I hope."

I laugh, grateful for her lightening of the mood. "Hilarious. I was thinking of the blue sundress with the white cardigan. Nothing fancy."

"Perfect," she approves. "Casual but cute. Fire chief approved."

The rest of my morning passes quickly with festival responsibilities—confirming vendor checkout procedures, reviewing clean-up schedules, finalizing the baking contest winners' press release for the local newspaper. By afternoon, I'm ready for a break from clipboard duties and decide to visit my grandmother at Sunset Pines.

Martha Barrett is having one of her good days, I'm pleased to discover. She recognizes me immediately, greeting me with a warm smile as I enter her room.

"Annie, dear," she says, patting the chair beside her. "Come, tell me about the festival. Did you win the baking contest?"

I laugh, settling beside her. "Grandma, I organized the contest. I couldn't enter it myself."

"Why not?" she asks, genuinely puzzled. "Your pies would have won, hands down."

"Conflict of interest," I explain. "But Mrs. Henderson's strawberry-rhubarb took Best in Show. You'd have approved. Her crust was perfect."

This launches a detailed discussion of proper pie crust technique, my grandmother slipping seamlessly into her role as a baking mentor despite her failing memory. These moments are precious—glimpses of the sharp-minded woman who raised me, who taught me everything I know about baking and business.

"Now," she says when we've exhausted the topic of pie, "tell me about Jake Colton."

The abrupt shift startles me. "What about him?"

"Don't play coy," she chides gently. "The nurses have been gossiping about you two dancing at the Spring Ball. Said you looked like something from a fairy tale."

News travels fast in Firelight Falls, particularly to places like Sunset Pines where gossip is a primary form of entertainment. "We danced," I acknowledge. "It's tradition for the fire chief and the baking contest coordinator."

"Mmm-hmm," she hums, unconvinced. "And is that why you were looking at him like he hung the moon? Tradition?"

I laugh. "You always could see right through me."

"Since you were a little girl," she agrees. "So? Are you and Jake finding your way back to each other?"

"We're trying," I tell her. "It's complicated. We're different people now."

"Love is always complicated," she says with the wisdom of her eighty-eight years. "Doesn't make it any less worth pursuing."

"I'm not sure if it's love," I protest, though the denial sounds weak even to my ears.

My grandmother fixes me with a knowing look. "Annie Barrett, that boy was your first love, and you never quite got over him. I knew it when you were twenty-two, and I know it now."

"I thought I had," I admit. "Moved on, I mean. Built a life without him."

"You built a life," she acknowledges. "A good one. Full of purpose and accomplishment. But there's always been a corner of your heart closed off, waiting for him to come back and claim it."

Her observation leaves me momentarily speechless. Have I been waiting for Jake all these years? Not consciously, perhaps, but in some deep, unacknowledged part of myself?

"He hurt me," I remind her softly.

"Yes," she agrees. "And now he's trying to make amends. The question is, are you brave enough to let him?"

Before I can respond, a nurse appears in the doorway.

"Ms. Barrett? There's a call for you at the front desk. Something about the lantern release tonight?"

I rise, squeezing my grandmother's hand. "Duty calls. I'll visit again soon."

"Be happy, Annie," she says, her eyes suddenly clearer and more focused than they've been in months. "Life's too short for anything else."

With her words echoing in my mind, I make my way to the front desk, where the receptionist hands me the phone. It's Mayor Wilson calling about a last-minute change to the lantern release program.

"We'd like you to join Chief Colton in releasing the first lanterns," he explains. "As our baking contest coordinator and a key member of the festival committee."

"That's traditionally the fire chief's role," I argue, surprised by the suggestion.

"Traditions evolve," the mayor says cheerfully. "Besides, the two of you made such a striking pair at the opening dance, the committee thought it would be fitting to have you launch the festival's closing event together as well."

I suspect the "committee" consists primarily of Firelight Falls' most dedicated matchmakers, but the mayor's enthusiasm is difficult to refuse. "If Chief Colton has no objection, I'd be honored," I concede.

"Excellent!" Mayor Wilson sounds pleased with himself. "The ceremony begins at eight. Be at the waterfall park by seven-thirty for a brief rehearsal."

After hanging up, I check my phone, finding no messages from Jake. His mother's situation must be requiring his full attention. I send a quick text.

> Hope everything's okay with your mom. Just got a call from Mayor Wilson about joining you for the first lantern release tonight. Let me know if that works for you.

I push down a twinge of worry when Jake doesn't respond, and head back to the festival grounds to complete my remaining responsibilities.

The afternoon passes in a blur of activity. By six o'clock, I'm back at my apartment, preparing for the evening's event. True to my plan, I choose the blue sundress and white cardigan, practical yet pretty for an outdoor event. The weather forecast promises a mild evening, perfect for the lantern release.

Still no word from Jake, which concerns me. I try calling his cell, but it goes straight to voicemail. Remembering his phone battery died earlier, I try not to worry. His mother's condition likely requires his undivided attention.

At seven-fifteen, I drive to the waterfall park, where festival-goers are already gathering in anticipation of the lantern release. The area has been transformed with twinkling lights and lantern stations where attendees can collect their paper lanterns and receive safety instructions from firefighters.

I spot Chief Williams near the main stage and approach him. "Evening, Chief. Have you seen Jake?"

Williams looks surprised by my question. "Not since this morning. He called to say he had a family situation and asked me to oversee final preparations. Is something wrong?"

"No, no," I assure him, though uncertainty gnaws at me. "Just haven't been able to reach him. Mayor Wilson wants me to join him for the first lantern release."

"Ah." Williams nods, understanding dawning. "Well, if I see him, I'll let him know you're looking for him."

I thank him and continue toward the stage area, where Mayor Wilson is conferring with other officials. He brightens when he sees me.

"Annie! Perfect timing. We were just finalizing the ceremony sequence."

"Has Chief Colton arrived?" I ask, glancing around.

The mayor checks his watch with a frown. "Not yet, but there's still time. He's probably just running late with festival duties."

I don't correct his assumption, not wanting to share Jake's private family matters. Instead, I listen as he explains the revised ceremony—welcome speech, brief history of the lantern tradition, demonstration of proper release technique, and then the first lanterns are released, symbolizing the official close of the festival's seventy-fifth year.

By seven forty-five, the park is filled with spectators, families spread on blankets near the waterfall, couples strolling hand-in-hand along illuminated pathways. The atmosphere is festive yet peaceful, a community united in celebration.

And still no sign of Jake.

My phone rings. I look at the display and see that it's Caroline calling.

"Annie?" she says as I accept the call.

"Caroline," I say, surprised. "I have been trying to reach Jake. Is everything okay?"

A brief hesitation before she responds. "Mom took a bad turn this afternoon. We're at Firelight Falls Memorial. The doctors are running tests now."

My heart sinks at this news. "I'm so sorry. Is there anything I can do?"

"Jake wanted me to call you," she continues. "He wouldn't be able to make it to the lantern release tonight. He feels terrible about it, but—"

"Of course," I interrupt. "His mother needs him. Please tell him not to worry about the festival. It's taken care of. I will inform the mayor that he won't be able to make it."

"Thank you. I will pass on the message. I know he's been looking forward to being at the ceremony with you."

The disappointment in her voice mirrors my own. "It's fine," I assure her, deciding not to tell her we were supposed to release the lanterns together. It would just make Jake feel worse about missing it. After ending the call, I seek out Mayor Wilson to explain the situation. He's understanding but flustered by the last-minute change.

"We've been advertising the fire chief releasing the first lantern," he frets. "It's tradition."

"Chief Williams can do it," I suggest. "As Jake's second-in-command."

"But the program already lists Chief Colton," the mayor points out. "The commemorative programs we printed yesterday."

I suppress a sigh at his fixation on this detail. "I'm sure no one will mind the substitution under the circumstances."

Before the mayor can respond, a familiar voice calls my name. I turn to see Ben Martinez approaching in his police uniform, looking concerned.

"Annie," he says as he reaches us. "Just heard about Chief Colton's mother. Tough situation."

"Yes," I agree. "He's at the hospital with her now."

"Which leaves us without our fire chief for the lantern release," Mayor Wilson interjects. "A significant problem for our ceremony."

Ben glances between us, assessing the situation. "I could step in," he offers, "as head of public safety in Chief Colton's absence. It would maintain the symbolism of safety officials leading the release."

The mayor sighs. "That will work. Deputy Martinez and Ms. Barrett releasing the first lanterns. Safety and community partnership represented beautifully."

Before I can object, the mayor hurries off to inform the stage manager of the change. Ben turns to me with an apologetic smile.

"Hope you don't mind the substitution," he says. "Seemed like the simplest solution."

"Not at all," I assure him, grateful for his practical approach. "Thank you for stepping in."

As eight o'clock approaches, festival workers distribute the ceremonial lanterns—beautiful biodegradable paper creations featuring the town seal and "75th Anniversary" in elegant script. Ben and I receive special gold-trimmed versions for the first release.

Mayor Wilson takes the stage, microphone in hand, to welcome the assembled crowd. His speech covers the festival's history, the significance of the lantern release, and gratitude to all who made the event possible.

"And now," he announces, "to officially close our seventy-fifth Spring Bloom Festival, please welcome Deputy Ben Martinez and our baking contest coordinator, Annie Barrett, who will release the first lanterns!"

Applause ripples through the crowd as Ben and I step onto the small platform overlooking the waterfall. Festival workers light our lanterns, the small fuel cells casting a warm glow through the delicate paper.

"Make a wish," Ben murmurs beside me as we prepare to release them.

I close my eyes briefly, thinking of Jake at the hospital with his mother, the dance we shared last night, and the possibilities unfolding between us. I wish for health and peace for those I love, and the courage to embrace what comes next.

"Ready?" Ben asks.

I nod, and together we release our lanterns into the evening sky. They rise slowly at first, then with gathering speed, golden light ascending above the waterfall. Around us, the crowd releases their own lanterns, until hundreds of glowing points of light float upward, a constellation of community hopes and wishes.

It's beautiful, magical even, yet I can't help feeling a pang of regret that Jake isn't here to share it.

Two hours later, as the festivities wrap up, I thank Ben for his help and make my way through the dispersing crowd toward the parking area. My festival duties are complete, and I'm eager to check on Jake and his mother, and offer whatever support I can.

The drive to Firelight Falls Memorial Hospital takes only ten minutes, but it feels longer with worry gnawing at me. I've heard nothing from Jake since Caroline's brief call hours ago, and the silence feels ominous somehow.

At the hospital's information desk, I ask to visit Mrs. Colton. The receptionist, a middle-aged woman with kind eyes, checks her computer.

"I'm sorry, but visiting hours ended at nine," she tells me. "Family only after that."

"I'm..." I hesitate, unsure how to define my relationship. "I'm close to the family. Jake—Chief Colton—he's my..."

The words stick in my throat. Boyfriend? Partner? We haven't really defined what we are.

"I understand," the receptionist says gently. "Perhaps you could try calling tomorrow?"

My heart sinks. "Is she okay? The patient, I mean?"

"I can't share medical details with non-family members," she explains apologetically. "I'm sorry."

I thank her and walk back to my car, feeling helpless and shut out. In the parking lot, I try calling Jake's cell phone. It rings several times before going to voicemail.

"Hi, it's me," I say after the beep. "I just tried to visit the hospital, but they said no visitors tonight. I hope your mother is okay. I'm thinking about you. Call me when you can."

I try Caroline's number next, but it also goes to voicemail.

At home, I pace my apartment, unable to settle. I try Jake's number again an hour later, then again before bed. Each call goes straight to voicemail now, as if his phone has been turned off.

Finally, as I'm brushing my teeth, my phone chimes with a text message. Relief floods through me—finally, word from Jake.

But when I read the message, confusion replaces relief.

> Jake: Mom's stable for now. Thanks for your concern, but we're handling this as a family. I'll be in touch when things settle down.

I stare at the screen, reading the words again. It's like receiving a message from a polite stranger rather than the man who held me close on the dance floor just last night.

Thanks for your concern? As if I'm a casual acquaintance rather than someone who cares deeply about him and his family.

I type a response several times, then delete each attempt. Something has shifted, but I don't understand what or why. The warmth between us seems to have evaporated in the space of a few hours.

Finally, I send a simple reply.

I'm here if you need anything. Thinking of you.

No response comes.

As I lie in bed, staring at the ceiling, my mind churns with possibilities. Is his mother worse than Caroline thought? Is Jake overwhelmed by family responsibilities and pulling back to focus on them? Or have I somehow misread the signals between us, assuming we were becoming more than just friends?

The thought that hurts most is the possibility that when faced with a genuine crisis, Jake has reverted to handling problems alone rather than accepting support from those who care about him.

Just like twenty years ago, when he disappeared rather than let me help with his father's troubles.

No, I tell myself firmly. Jake's changed. We've both changed. This is just stress, just a difficult situation. Tomorrow will be better.

# *Jake*

HOSPITALS AT NIGHT ARE strange—a hush punctuated by electronic beeps, fluorescent lights that never dim completely, the squeak of rubber-soled shoes on linoleum floors. I've spent too many nights in settings like this with injured firefighters, with Lisa during her illness, and now with my mother.

Her room is dimly lit, machines monitoring her vital signs as she sleeps, medication finally bringing relief from the agitation that had consumed her earlier. Caroline left an hour ago, exhausted but reassured by the doctor that our mother had suffered a TIA—a mini-stroke—but was now stable and expected to recover.

I should feel relieved too. Should be focused entirely on my mother's health, on what this episode means for her care. Instead, I'm drowning in memories I thought I'd buried, overwhelmed by the familiar weight of watching someone I love slip away piece by piece.

Being in the hospital with Mom brought back memories of Lisa in her hospital bed, her gradual decline, and the helpless feeling of watching a person you love disappear before your eyes. The bone-deep exhaustion of being strong for everyone else while falling apart inside.

I can't do this again.

I've been so focused on reconnecting with Annie, on building something new between us, that I haven't allowed myself to fully process what I'm risking. Not just my heart, but my ability to be the father Maddie needs.

My phone buzzes—a voicemail from Annie. I can hear the concern in her voice as she explains about trying to visit, about wanting to be here for our family. The word "family" should warm me. Instead, it sends a spike of panic through my chest.

Our family. As if she's already part of it, already woven into the fabric of our lives so deeply that losing her would tear us apart.

Just like losing Lisa tore us apart.

I remember those first months after Lisa's funeral. The crushing weight of grief. The way simple tasks became monumental challenges. Getting Maddie to school, making meals, and trying to function at work was nearly impossible. If Caroline hadn't stepped in...

And Maddie. God, what did I put her through? A twelve-year-old girl who'd just lost her mother, watching her father struggle to hold himself together. On the nights I thought she was asleep, she was probably listening to me fall apart in the next room.

I pulled myself together eventually, for her sake, but it took everything I had. Every ounce of strength I possessed.

What if I open my heart completely to Annie and life takes her away too? Cancer, accidents, any of the thousand things that can destroy a life in an instant? Would I be strong enough to survive it a second time? Would I be able to hold it together for Maddie, or would I completely shatter?

My mother stirs in her sleep, muttering something I can't quite make out. I study her face, seeing echoes of the vibrant woman she once was before my father's drinking and gambling broke her spirit. She never really recovered from losing him. Even though their marriage was troubled, the love was real; when he died, something in her died too.

The Colton family and love, I think bitterly. We don't have a great track record.

Another buzz from my phone—Annie again. She's trying to be supportive, to step into this crisis with us. Just like she would if we were truly together, truly committed. Just like she would if she loved me.

And that's the problem. Because I'm falling in love with her again—have already fallen, if I'm honest. Not the desperate, all-consuming love of our youth, but something deeper, more mature and far more devastating to lose.

I think about Maddie at Caroline's house, probably worried about her grandmother, maybe wondering why I haven't called. She's old enough to understand more than I'd like her to about adult problems. Old enough to see through any facade I might try to maintain.

She's been so good about Annie, so accepting of our growing relationship. But what happens if Annie becomes truly integral to our family and then something happens to her? What happens to Maddie if she has to watch me break apart again?

I can't put her through that. I won't put her through that.

You can't live your life in fear of loss. Annie is healthy, young, and there's no reason to assume the worst, the rational part of my brain argues.

But life doesn't follow rational patterns. Lisa was healthy too... until she wasn't. Young, until cancer aged her decades in months. The randomness of tragedy is what makes it so terrifying.

My fingers hover over my phone, Annie's messages still unanswered. I know what I should do—call her back, let her be here for us, allow our relationship to deepen naturally. Trust in what we're building.

Instead, I decide to send a text. It's safer that way. Less emotional.

> Mom's stable for now. Thanks for your concern, but we're handling this as a family. I'll be in touch when things settle down.

I stare at the message before sending it, knowing it will hurt her, knowing it contradicts everything I've promised about communication and trust. But the protective instinct for myself and Maddie overrides rational thought.

Better to step back now, before we're all in too deep. Before Maddie gets more attached. Before I risk everything on a love that life could snatch away without warning.

I hit send before I can change my mind.

Her response comes quickly.

> Annie: I'm here if you need anything. Thinking of you.

The message makes my chest tight with guilt and longing. Of course, she's here. Of course, she's offering support without conditions, without resentment. Because she's Annie, and she loves with her whole heart.

Which is exactly why I need to protect us all from this.

A soft knock at the door interrupts my thoughts. A nurse enters, checking monitors and adjusting my mother's IV while trying not to disturb her.

"You should try to get some rest," she says, noting my position in the uncomfortable visitor's chair. "We can bring in a cot if you're planning to stay."

"Thank you," I say gratefully. "That would be helpful."

After she leaves, I check my phone again. No new messages from Annie, though I hadn't really expected any after my curt reply. There is, however, a text from Maddie.

> **Maddie:** Everything okay with Grandma? How's Annie? Aunt Caroline said there was a medical thing?

> Grandma stable, doctors optimistic. Annie's fine. How are you doing at Caroline's?

I sigh. Already she's asking about Annie. I can't let this go any further and risk her really getting hurt again.

> Good. Homework done. Watching old movies with Aunt C. When will you be home?

My heart squeezes in my chest. My girl, always so strong and independent. I wonder what her mother would think of the job I've done since she left us.

> Tomorrow morning. Get some sleep. Love you.

Setting my phone aside, I lean back in the uncomfortable chair, closing my eyes against the hospital's muted lighting. The weight of my decision sits heavy on my chest, but I tell myself it's the right one. The responsible one.

I've survived loss before. I can survive pulling back from Annie now, before it's too late. Before I risk losing myself so completely that I can't be the father Maddie needs.

The nurse returns with a folding cot, setting it up along the wall of my mother's room. I thank her again, grateful for the hospital's accommodation.

"Your girlfriend called earlier," she mentions casually. "While you were with the doctor. She seemed worried about your mother. Sweet of her to check in."

"She's..." I start, then stop. What is Annie to me now? Someone I'm pushing away to protect us both? "She's a good friend."

The nurse nods approvingly. "It's nice when people care. Your mother's lucky to have so many people looking out for her."

After she leaves, guilt washes over me in waves. Annie cared enough to call the hospital to check on my mother's condition. She tried to visit, to offer support, to be there for our family. And I responded by shutting her out.

But what's the alternative? Let her get pulled deeper into our family's medical drama? Let Maddie become more attached to someone who might not be permanent? Let myself fall so completely in love that losing her would destroy me?

I stretch out on the cot, physically and emotionally drained. The last forty-eight hours have been a rollercoaster between the high of the Spring Ball and the low of finding out my mother had declined. I'm exhausted.

My mind won't stop racing long enough for me to fall asleep. What am I doing, really? Twenty years ago, a family emergency led me to make a decision that separated us for decades. Now, another family crisis is making me want to create distance again.

But this time, I tell myself, I'm not running away to protect Annie from my problems. I'm pulling back to protect all of us from the devastation that comes when love ends.

Some people are strong enough to love regardless of the risk. To open their hearts again and again, no matter how many times life breaks them. But I'm not so sure I'm one of those people. And I won't risk finding out at the expense of my daughter's stability.

As sleep finally claims me, my last conscious thought is of Annie. The thought of seeing the light in her eyes extinguished, of going through that devastation again, is more than I can bear.

I can't do it. Even if protecting myself means breaking both our hearts.

# Annie

Monday mornings at the bakery are typically quiet, giving us a chance to restock, clean, and prepare for the week ahead after the rush of the weekend. Today, the usual peace is disrupted by my restless mind. The events of last night are playing in my mind on a loop.

The lantern release. Jake's absence. His mother's health scare. The brief, emotionless text about handling things "as a family."

"You've wiped that same counter three times now," Lana observes, interrupting my thoughts. "Pretty sure it's clean."

I glance down at the rag in my hand, surprised to find myself at the front counter. "Just being thorough," I mumble.

Lana steps closer, lowering her voice though we're alone in the bakery. "Have you heard from him this morning?"

"Not yet," I admit, checking my phone for what feels like the hundredth time. "But his mother's in the hospital. He's got enough to worry about without—"

"Without shutting out the woman who loves him?" Lana finishes bluntly. "Annie, I love you, but sometimes your willingness to make excuses for everyone else drives me crazy."

"I'm not making excuses," I protest, though even as I say it, I know it's not entirely true. "His mother had a stroke, Lana. Of course, his focus is on family right now."

"And you're not family?" she counters. "After everything you two have rebuilt together? After the way Maddie has embraced you?"

The question hits harder than I'd like to admit. Last night, when Jake texted they were "handling this as a family," the exclusion had stung more than I'd allowed myself to acknowledge. After weeks of growing closer, his instinct had been to shut me out.

"We're not married," I say weakly. "Not even officially engaged. We're just—"

"In love," Lana interrupts. "Completely, obviously in love. But if he's going to pull away every time life gets complicated, maybe you need to ask yourself if this is really what you want."

Before I can respond, the bell above the door chimes, signaling our first customer of the day. I plaster on a professional smile, grateful for the distraction, but Lana's words echo in my mind throughout the morning.

The day passes slowly, each hour without contact from Jake adding weight to the growing knot in my stomach. By lunch, I've convinced myself that something must be wrong—his mother's condition has worsened, or there's been another emergency. But when I finally break down and text Caroline, her response is brief but telling.

> Caroline: Mom's stable. Being discharged this afternoon. Jake's being Jake—brooding and stubborn.

So, it's not about his mother's health. It's about Jake retreating into himself, just like he did twenty years ago when faced with a family crisis. The realization brings a familiar ache, the echo of old wounds I thought we'd healed.

Just as I'm closing the bakery that afternoon, Caroline appears at my door, looking tired but determined. Her designer clothes are wrinkled, her usually perfect hair is a mess, and she removes her sunglasses to reveal eyes shadowed with exhaustion.

"How is your mother?" I ask as I let her in.

"Better. Home now, with a care plan in place." Caroline's voice is steady, but I can hear the underlying strain. "The doctors are optimistic about her recovery. She's got a long road ahead of her, though."

"Thank goodness she'll be okay," I say sincerely. "And Jake? How is he holding up?"

Caroline's expression tightens. "That's why I'm here. My brother is being an idiot."

The bluntness of her words surprises a laugh out of me. "Tell me what you really think."

"He's convinced himself that getting closer to you puts Maddie at risk of more loss," Caroline explains, settling into one of the cafe chairs. "That if something happens to you—or if you decide you don't want the complications of his life—it will devastate her."

My heart clenches. "So he's pulling away to protect her."

"To protect all of you, supposedly," Caroline says with obvious frustration. "Though mostly I think he's protecting himself. Twenty years ago, he ran to protect you, but in part, I think it was to protect his pride. He didn't want to drag you into our unsavory family mess. Now... he's running scared."

"But he's not running," I point out. "He's here in Firelight Falls."

"Physically, yes. Emotionally?" Caroline shakes her head. "He's building walls as fast as he can. Told me this morning that maybe it would be better if you two 'took a step back' while he focuses on family responsibilities."

Nausea hits hard and fast. After everything we've shared, everything we've built together, Jake is ready to throw it away at the first sign of complications. Just like before.

"I see," I manage, my voice steadier than I feel.

Caroline leans forward, her expression intense. "Annie, I need you to understand something. My brother loves you. He is completely, desperately in love with you. But he's terrified of loss in a way that's not entirely rational."

"Because of Lisa," I mumble.

"Because of Lisa, because of our father, because of twenty years of believing he has to carry everything alone." Caroline's voice grows more passionate. "He watched Lisa die slowly, watched Maddie grieve, barely held himself together through all of it. The idea of risking that kind of devastation again—or putting Maddie through it—is paralyzing him."

I understand the logic, even though it breaks my heart. "So what am I supposed to do? Wait for him to decide I'm worth the risk? Step back and just be friends? I have to be honest here. I don't know if I can do that. I'm not sure what you want me to do here."

"Fight for him," Caroline says simply. "Don't let him disappear into his protective shell without making him see what he's throwing away."

"I can't force him to want me in his life, Caroline."

"But you can make sure he knows what life without you actually means," she counters. "Right now, he's operating on fear and hypotheticals. Maybe it's time for some reality."

Before I can ask what she means, Caroline reaches into her purse and withdraws a familiar wooden box. My breath catches as she places it on the table between us.

"What's this?"

"Jake's letters," Caroline says. "Apparently, he wrote to you even when he didn't reach out." She rolls her eyes. "Because even when he let you go, he couldn't truly let you go."

My hands tremble as I reach for the box. "He wants me to have these now?"

Caroline's expression softens. "He told me he was going to give them to you yesterday, before Mom's episode. Said it was time you knew what these twenty years really looked like from his perspective. After last night"—she shakes her head —"I don't know if he'll be smart enough to give them to you."

"So you're taking matters into your own hands?"

"Someone has to," Caroline says firmly. "My brother is about to make the same mistake twice, and I won't let him destroy the best thing that's ever happened to him because he's too scared to live."

I clutch the box to my chest, feeling the weight of twenty years of unshared thoughts, unspoken feelings. "What if reading these just makes everything hurt more?"

"Then at least you'll hurt with the full truth," Caroline says gently. "At least you'll know exactly what you're fighting for."

After Caroline leaves, I sit alone in my empty bakery, staring at the wooden box. Part of me wants to open it immediately, to devour two decades of Jake's private thoughts. Another part fears I'll find that our reconnection meant as much to him as it did to me, making his current withdrawal even more painful.

In the end, I decide to wait. I lock the box in my office and finish my closing routine, trying to push down the growing certainty that Jake is slipping away from me again, just when I thought we'd finally found our way back to each other.

That night, I lie awake in my bed, staring at the ceiling and wondering if loving Jake Colton will always mean losing him to his own fears. Wondering if some patterns are too deep to break, no matter how much love exists between two people.

Wondering if this time, I'll be strong enough to let him go if that's what it takes to protect my heart.

# Jake

THREE DAYS AFTER BRINGING Mom home from the hospital, I'm sitting in my office at the fire station, staring at paperwork I can't focus on. Every time I try to concentrate on budget reports or training schedules, my mind drifts to Annie. I keep imagining the hurt she must have felt when I told her we needed space. The way she'd stopped calling or texting after I told her that family had to come first.

Family has to come first.

The phrase has become my mantra, my justification for pulling back from the best thing that's happened to me in years. But even as I repeat it, I know it's not entirely honest. This isn't really about putting family first—it's about protecting myself from the devastation that nearly destroyed me when Lisa died. I loved her completely. Had given our marriage everything I had, but the love I have for Annie... it's different. I don't think I'd survive losing her, too.

A knock on my office door interrupts my brooding. "Come in."

I expect Chief Williams or one of the guys, but instead, Maddie appears in the doorway, still in her school clothes, her backpack slung over one shoulder.

"Hey, sweetheart," I say, surprised. "What are you doing here? I thought you were going home with Sarah after school."

"I was," she says, closing the door behind her and settling into the chair across from my desk. "But I needed to talk to you."

She's serious, a determined look on her face, very unlike her usual teenage casualness, and it immediately puts me on alert. "Everything okay? Is it Grandma?"

"Grandma's fine. She's probably napping." Maddie studies me with an intensity that reminds me uncomfortably of her mother. "This is about you being an idiot."

"Excuse me?"

"You heard me." She crosses her arms, clearly prepared for battle. "You're pushing Annie away because you're scared, and it's stupid."

Heat rises in my chest—partly embarrassment at being called out by my fifteen-year-old daughter, partly defensive anger. "Maddie, you don't understand the situation—"

"I understand perfectly," she interrupts. "You're in love with Annie. She's in love with you. But instead of being happy about it, you're freaking out because what if something bad happens to her? What if she leaves? What if I get hurt if things don't work out?"

I'm momentarily speechless because, apparently, I can't keep anything from this brilliant girl of mine. "It's more complicated than that."

"No, it's not." Maddie leans forward, her young face fierce with conviction. "Dad, do you remember what you told me after Mom died? When I said I never wanted to love anyone again because losing people hurts too much?"

I remember—one of many late-night conversations during those awful first months of grief. "I told you that love is always worth the risk."

"You said that not loving to avoid being hurt was like not living to avoid dying," she continues. "That the pain of loss doesn't erase the joy of love—it proves how precious love is."

My own words, thrown back at me by my daughter, hit hard. "That's different—"

"How?" she demands. "How is it different when it's you instead of me? How is it different when it's Annie instead of some theoretical future boyfriend I might have?"

I struggle for an answer, for some way to explain the crushing weight of responsibility I feel, the terror of watching another person I love slip away. "Because you're fifteen, and I'm your father, and I can't—I can't fall apart again if something happens. You need me to be strong."

Maddie's expression softens slightly, but her resolve doesn't waver. She puts her hand on mine and says, "Dad, you didn't fall apart when Mom died. You grieved, yeah. You struggled. But you never fell apart. You were there for me every single day, even when I could tell you were dying inside."

"Maddie—"

"And Annie isn't Mom," she continues quietly. "She's not sick. She's not going anywhere. Annie's healthy, and she loves us, and she makes you happier than I've seen you since before Mom got cancer."

The truth in her words is undeniable, but it doesn't ease the fear that's been gnawing at me since Mom's stroke. "What if something happens to her? What if—"

"Then we'll deal with it," Maddie says. "Together. Like we always do. But Dad, you can't live your life expecting the worst thing to happen. That's not protecting me—that's teaching me to be afraid of happiness."

Her insight floors me. Is that what I'm doing? Teaching my daughter that love isn't worth the risk, that safety lies in emotional distance?

"She makes you laugh," Maddie adds, her voice growing gentler. "Really laugh, not just the polite dad-laugh you do when people tell jokes that aren't funny. She makes you sing in the car again. She made you start wearing that cologne you used to wear when you and Mom would go on dates."

I hadn't realized Maddie had noticed any of those things, these small ways Annie had brought me back to life.

"And she's good for me too," my daughter continues. "She doesn't try to be Mom—she's just Annie. She listens when I talk about Mom, doesn't get weird when I mention her. She helped me with that English essay about family traditions, the one where I wrote about Mom's Christmas cookies. Remember? She even helped me make them exactly the way Mom used to."

I remember. Annie had spent an entire Saturday afternoon with Maddie, working through Lisa's handwritten recipe, making batch after batch until they got it right. I'd found them flour-dusted and laughing in my kitchen, the house smelling like my late wife's Christmas cookies for the first time since she died.

"She's not trying to replace Mom," Maddie says, reading my thoughts. "She's just... adding to our family. Making it bigger instead of trying to make it different."

She's right. Annie has never tried to erase Lisa's presence from our lives—instead, she's found ways to honor it while creating space for new love, new traditions, new happiness.

"I love her, Dad," Maddie says quietly, "not like I loved Mom, but in her own way. And I love seeing you happy again. Really happy, not just okay."

My throat tightens with emotion. "Sweetheart—"

"Don't mess this up," she interrupts, her voice fierce again. "Don't let fear make you throw away something amazing. Mom wouldn't want that for you. She'd want you to grab happiness with both hands and hold on tight."

The truth of that statement nearly undoes me. Lisa, in her last weeks, had made me promise to live fully after she was gone, to find love again if I could, to give Maddie an example of resilience and hope rather than fear and withdrawal.

"What if I hurt Annie?" I ask quietly. "What if I'm not ready for this? What if I screw it up again?"

Maddie rolls her eyes. "Then you apologize and do better. That's what adults do, right? They mess up and learn and try again?"

Another echo of my own parenting philosophy, delivered with a teenage attitude that makes me want to laugh and cry simultaneously.

"Besides," she adds with a slight smile, "I think Annie's pretty tough. She survived twenty years without you, built her own life, and opened a successful business. I don't think she's going to crumble if you have some moments of being dumb."

Annie can handle whatever complications my life might bring.

"You really think I should fight for her?" I ask.

"I think you should stop fighting yourself," Maddie says. "Annie's not going anywhere unless you push her away. And pushing away someone who loves you because you're afraid of losing them is the dumbest thing ever."

I lean back in my chair, overwhelmed by my daughter's wisdom. "When did you get so smart?" I ask.

"Good genes," she says with a grin that reminds me of Lisa. "Plus, I've been watching you and Annie for weeks. It's pretty obvious you're crazy about each other."

"Is it really that obvious?"

"Dad, you light up like a Christmas tree every time she texts you. And she gets this dopey smile whenever someone mentions your name. It's kind of gross, actually, but also really sweet."

I can't help but laugh. "Thanks for the assessment."

"So what are you going to do?" Maddie asks, leaning forward expectantly.

The answer comes to me with sudden clarity. "I'm going to grovel."

"Good," she says, standing and shouldering her backpack. "And Dad? Do it soon. Aunt Caroline said Annie's pretty hurt by you pulling away."

Guilt crashes over me as I realize how my fear-driven withdrawal must have appeared to Annie—like history repeating itself, like the boy who ran away twenty years ago doing it again when things got complicated.

"You're right," I admit. "I've been an idiot."

"The biggest," Maddie agrees cheerfully. "But you're my idiot, and I love you. Even when you make terrible decisions."

After she leaves, I sit in my office for a long time, thinking about everything she said. About love and risk, about teaching by example, about the difference between protecting the people you love and protecting yourself from loving them.

About the woman who has brought light back into my life, who has embraced my daughter and my complications with open arms, who deserves so much better than a man too afraid of his own heart to fight for what matters most.

It's time to stop running from happiness. Time to stop letting fear make my decisions.

Time to win back the woman I should never have pushed away.

# Annie

THURSDAY EVENING FINDS ME in my apartment, curled up on my couch with the wooden box of letters open beside me. I've been reading them for hours, working my way chronologically through twenty years of Jake's unspoken thoughts, his struggles, his feelings for me, even as he built a life with someone else.

The early letters are raw with pain and regret, filled with explanations for why he left, promises to return, desperate hope I might wait for him. Then come the letters documenting his life in Houston—his training as a firefighter, his growing relationship with Lisa, his wrestling with guilt over moving forward while still loving me.

I met someone today, one letter begins, dated nearly four years after he left. Her name is Lisa...

I have to stop reading at that point, overwhelmed by the complex mix of emotions I'm feeling. There's pain, but also a kind of peace. Reading about Jake's journey toward love with Lisa doesn't diminish what we had. It helps me understand the depth of his capacity for love.

The later letters chronicle his marriage, Maddie's birth, and his rising career. Each milestone shared with me in these unsent pages, as if some part of him couldn't bear for me not to witness his journey. The love for his family is clear in every word, but so is the persistent ache of our unfinished story.

Then come the letters about Lisa's illness, and my heart breaks for the fear and helplessness he must have felt.

I think of you, he writes, wondering if you're happy, if life has been kind to you. Hoping that wherever you are, whatever you're doing, you're surrounded by love and happiness.

By the time I reach the last letter—written just weeks before his return to Firelight Falls—tears are streaming down my face. Not just for the pain in his words, but for the beautiful, complicated, enduring love they reveal. A love that survived twenty years of separation, that carried us both through other relationships and loss, that somehow led us back to each other.

You have been, in some essential way, my true north, he writes. The standard against which I've measured integrity, courage, and love itself.

I close the box with trembling hands, overwhelmed by the gift Jake has given me—an unfiltered window into his soul, this record of a heart that never let me go completely.

A soft knock at my door interrupts my thoughts. I wipe my tears quickly, assuming it's Lana checking on me, but when I open the door, I find Jake standing in my hallway, looking uncertain and slightly desperate. He's holding a bouquet of wildflowers—daisies and black-eyed Susans and Queen Anne's lace—their stems uneven, some petals missing, clearly picked rather than purchased.

"Hi," he says.

"Hi," I reply, my heart hammering against my ribs. Four days of silence, four days of wondering if he was going to disappear from my life again, and now he's here, looking like a man who's been wrestling with demons.

"These are for you," he continues, offering the imperfect bouquet. "I know they're not much. I picked them from the side of the road on the way here. The florist was closed, and I didn't want to wait any longer to—"

"They're beautiful," I interrupt, accepting the flowers. "Thank you."

We stand there for a moment, the weight of everything unsaid hanging between us. Jake's eyes are circled with dark shadows.

"Can I come in?" he asks. "I know I don't deserve it after how I've behaved, but I need to explain. I need to—"

"Jake," I say gently, stepping back to let him enter. "You don't have to explain. I understand why you pulled away."

He follows me into my apartment, watching as I fill a vase with water for the wildflowers. "Do you? Because I'm not sure I understood it myself until today."

I turn to face him, taking in his rumpled appearance, the lines of stress around his eyes. "Your mother's health scare made you remember how quickly everything can change. How devastating loss can be. You're protecting yourself and Maddie from potential heartbreak."

A look of surprise crosses Jake's face. "You understand."

"Yes, I do." I settle into my armchair and gesture for him to take the couch. "But understanding and accepting are two different things."

He sits heavily, his shoulders sagging. "Annie, I'm sorry. I know I hurt you. I know pulling away after everything we've shared was unfair and—"

"It was terrifying," I interrupt, my composure cracking slightly. "Watching you retreat, feeling you shut down, seeing you choose fear over us—it brought back every feeling from twenty years ago. Like, no matter how much we love each other, no matter how strong our connection is, you'll always run when things get complicated."

Pain flashes across his face. "That's not—I wasn't running. I was trying to be responsible, to think about Maddie's needs—"

"By denying her the chance to have more love in her life?" I challenge gently. "By teaching her that love isn't worth the risk?"

Jake's mouth opens, then closes, as if my words have struck home in a way he wasn't expecting.

"I read your letters," I tell him, nodding toward the wooden box on my coffee table. "Caroline brought them to me. All of them."

His eyes widen. "All of them? But I thought—Caroline wasn't supposed to—"

"She was worried about you," I explain. "About us. She thought maybe if I understood your perspective, your journey, I might help you see past your fear."

Jake is quiet for a long moment, staring at the box. "What did you think? Of the letters?"

"I think they're beautiful," I say honestly. "Heartbreaking and honest and so completely you. They helped me understand that our connection wasn't lost, even when we were apart. What we're building now isn't just nostalgia or second chances—it's something that was always meant to be."

"Then you understand why losing you—or the possibility of losing you—terrifies me," he says.

"I understand the fear," I acknowledge. "But Jake, you can't live your life trying to prevent loss. You can't love halfway to avoid being hurt."

He runs his hands through his hair, a gesture I recognize from our youth. "Maddie said something similar. Called me an idiot for pushing away happiness because I was afraid of losing it."

I smile. "She's a wise girl."

"Too wise," he mutters. "She basically told me that not loving to avoid being hurt was like not living to avoid dying."

"Smart kid," I agree. "She gets that from her dad."

"Her dad's been an idiot," Jake says, looking at me directly for the first time since he arrived. "Her dad let fear make decisions that hurt the woman he loves more than life itself."

The words send a flutter through my chest, but I'm not ready to let him off the hook yet. "What changed? What made you come here tonight?"

"Maddie," he admits. "She cornered me at the station today, called me out for being scared and stupid. Reminded me of some advice I gave her after her mother died—about love being worth the risk, about not letting fear keep you from living fully."

"And you listened to her?"

"Eventually," he says with a rueful smile. "After she pointed out that I was teaching her to be afraid of happiness instead of protecting her from it."

I nod. "She's right. And Jake, if you're worried about how losing someone might affect Maddie—she's stronger than you think. She's already survived the worst loss a child can face. She knows how to grieve and heal and love again."

"I know that," he says. "Intellectually, I know all of this. But when Mom had her stroke, when I was sitting in that hospital watching her struggle, all I could think about was how fragile everything is. How quickly the people we love can be taken from us."

"And your solution was to take yourself away first?"

Jake winces. "When you put it like that, it sounds even more cowardly than it felt."

I lean forward, closing some of the distance between us. "Jake, I need you to hear something. I'm not going anywhere unless you push me away. But even if something happened to me—accident, illness, whatever—would you really rather have never loved me at all?"

He looks stricken by the question. "No. God, no. These weeks with you have brought me back to life in ways I didn't know I was missing."

"Then why are you willing to throw that away to avoid a hypothetical pain?"

"Because I'm a coward," he says simply. "Because losing Lisa nearly destroyed me, and the thought of going through that again, of putting Maddie through watching me fall apart again—"

"You didn't fall apart when Lisa died," I interrupt gently. "You grieved. You struggled. But you held it together for your daughter, you built a life for both of you, you survived and eventually thrived. You're stronger than you think, Jake."

He's quiet for a long moment, absorbing my words. When he speaks again, his voice is thick with emotion. "I love you, Annie. I love you so much it scares me. The thought of building a life together, of being happy, of having everything I want—and then losing it—"

"Terrifies you," I finish. "I understand. But Jake, the only guarantee in life is that it ends. We can't control when or how. All we can control is how fully we love while we're here."

"You make it sound so simple."

"It is simple," I say. "Not easy, but simple. Love me or don't love me. Be with me or don't be with me. But don't love me halfway because you're afraid of loving me completely. That's not fair to either of us."

Jake stands suddenly, beginning to pace my small living room. "I want to be with you. I want to love you completely. I want to build a life together, get married... I want all of it, Annie."

The admission sends warmth flooding through me. "Then what's stopping you?"

"The voice in my head that says I'm being selfish," he says. "That says I'm risking Maddie's emotional stability for my happiness, or that a good father would choose security over love."

"And what does your heart say?"

He stops pacing, meeting my eyes. "My heart says that Maddie deserves to see her father living fully, loving completely, embracing happiness when it comes. My heart says that loving you doesn't put her at risk—it gives her more love, more family, more examples of what healthy relationships look like."

"I say that your heart's right," I tell him softly.

"I know," he says, sinking back onto the couch. "I know that, but knowing and feeling are two different things. Annie, I don't know how to stop being afraid."

I stand and move to sit beside him on the couch, taking his hands in mine. "You don't have to stop being afraid. You just have to love me. Fear and love can exist in the same heart, Jake. They don't cancel each other out."

He looks down at our joined hands. "I hurt you. I pulled away when I should have pulled you closer. I made you doubt our relationship when I should have been fighting for it."

"Yes," I agree. "You did all of those things."

"How do I fix it?" he asks, his blue eyes vulnerable in a way that reminds me of the boy I fell in love with twenty years ago.

"By deciding what you want more—safety or love. Security or happiness. A life protected from potential pain, or a life lived fully despite the risks."

Jake is quiet for a long moment, and I can almost see him wrestling with himself, fear and love battling in his heart. Finally, he looks up at me.

"I want you," he says simply. "I want us. I want to build a life together and love you completely and face whatever comes knowing we're stronger together than apart."

"Even if it's scary?"

"Even if it's scary," he says with growing conviction. "Because loving you is worth it."

Relief and joy flood me as I see the man I love finally choosing love over fear. "Jake—"

"I'm not done," he interrupts, sliding off the couch to kneel before me. "Annie Barrett, I've been an idiot. I've let fear make decisions that nearly cost me everything that matters. I want to spend the rest of my life making up for the time I wasted being scared."

He reaches into his pocket and withdraws a small velvet box. "I bought this before Mom's stroke. I've been carrying it around, waiting for the perfect moment, the right words, the courage to ask you to be my wife."

My breath catches as he opens the box, revealing a gorgeous princess-cut diamond.

"I realize now that the perfect moment is any moment we're together. Annie, will you marry me? Will you take a chance on a man who's finally learned that love is always worth the risk?"

Through my tears, I see not just the man I love, but the future we can build together—complicated, imperfect, sometimes scary, but full of love and joy and the kind of happiness that comes from choosing each other every day.

"Yes," I whisper, then louder, "Yes, Jake Colton. I will marry you."

As he slides the ring onto my finger and pulls me into his arms, I feel the last of my doubts disappear. This is our second chance, our new beginning, our choice to love completely despite the risks.

And this time, we're both brave enough to choose love.

# Jake

Five months later, I stand in the community center's small side room, adjusting my tie and trying to calm my nerves. Outside, I can hear the gentle murmur of our guests arriving—family, friends, nearly half the town of Firelight Falls who have embraced our love story as their own.

"You're going to wear a hole in that tie if you keep fiddling with it," Caroline observes from the doorway, looking elegant in her deep blue bridesmaid dress.

"Just want everything to be perfect for her," I admit.

"It already is," Caroline assures me, crossing the room to straighten my tie properly. "Annie doesn't need perfect, Jake. She just needs you—the real you, including the nervous fidgeting."

Her words calm me somewhat. Annie and I had chosen a simple autumn wedding—close friends and family, minimal fuss, focus on commitment rather than spectacle. Yet somehow, the community had embraced our union as a cause for celebration, offering help and support that still amazes me.

"Everyone's seated," Caroline reports, stepping back to assess my appearance. "Mom's in the front row with Martha Barrett, both of them already teary-eyed. Your firefighters are lined up outside to form that honor arch thing. And Maddie's with Annie, putting the finishing touches on her bouquet."

"How is she?" I ask, referring to Annie. "Nervous?"

Caroline's smile softens. "Radiant. And more certain than I've ever seen anyone on their wedding day. Not a hint of cold feet or second thoughts."

Relief washes through me. After my fear-driven withdrawal, part of me still marvels that Annie gave me another chance, that she's willing to bind her life to mine despite my capacity for making stupid decisions when faced with a crisis.

"Good," I say, checking my watch. "Because I'm done running from happiness. Done letting fear make my choices."

"I know you are," Caroline says gently. "We all know you are. Including Annie."

A knock at the door interrupts us, and Chief Williams enters, looking distinguished in his formal uniform. As my best man, he's been a steady presence throughout our engagement, offering quiet support and occasional reality checks when needed.

"Ready, Jake?" he asks. "It's time."

I take a deep breath, thinking of the woman waiting for me at the altar, of the life we're about to begin together, of the family we're creating from love and choice and second chances.

"More than ready," I tell him honestly.

The community center's main hall has been transformed for the occasion—autumn leaves and warm lighting creating a golden atmosphere, simple white flowers adorning the aisle seats, a backdrop of copper and gold behind the altar where Mayor Wilson waits to officiate our ceremony.

As I take my position at the front of the room, I'm struck by the faces looking back at me—my firefighters in dress uniform, Annie's bakery customers turned friends, neighbors who've watched our love story unfold with interest and affection. This is our community, our chosen family, our support system.

The string quartet plays, and the small wedding party begins its processional. Caroline enters first as maid of honor, her expression radiant with joy for our happiness. She's followed by Maddie, who walked alone rather than serve as a traditional bridesmaid, carrying a single white rose in honor of her mother—a touch that had brought tears to my eyes when she suggested it.

My daughter catches my eye as she takes her place opposite Caroline, her smile bright with genuine happiness. The past months have been a period of change for all of us, but Maddie has embraced Annie's permanent place in our lives with grace and enthusiasm that still amazes me.

"You look good, Dad," she mouths, causing me to grin despite my nerves.

The music shifts, and the assembled guests rise as Annie appears in the doorway, radiant in her mermaid gown. Her grandmother, now in a wheelchair due to declining health, beams from the front row.

The sight of my bride steals my breath—not because of her dress, though it's gorgeous and fits her perfectly—but because of the joy and love radiating from her as our eyes meet across the room.

She moves toward me with elegance, kissing her grandmother's cheek before continuing to my side. When she reaches me, her hand slips into mine as naturally as breathing, our fingers interlacing in that familiar way that always feels like coming home.

"Hi," she whispers, eyes shining with emotion.

"Hi," I reply, my voice rough with feeling. "You're beautiful."

"You clean up pretty well yourself," she teases gently, and I can feel my
nerves settling in her presence.

Mayor Wilson clears his throat, bringing our attention back to the
ceremony. "Friends and family," he begins, his voice carrying easily
through the hall. "We are gathered today to witness the union of Annie
Barrett and Jake Colton—two people who have shown us that love is
patient, love is persistent, and that sometimes, it takes a scenic route to
find its way home."

Gentle laughter ripples through the audience at his apt description.
The mayor continues with remarks about community, commitment,
and the courage required to love fully despite life's uncertainties—words
that resonate deeply given our particular journey.

When he invites us to share our vows, I go first, taking both Annie's
hands in mine, my earlier nerves completely forgotten as I focus on the
woman who has brought me back to life.

"Annie," I begin, my voice steady. "I almost made the biggest mistake
of my life. I let fear convince me that loving you was selfish, that
protecting myself and Maddie from potential loss was more important
than embracing the happiness you brought to our lives."

Her eyes glisten with unshed tears as I continue. "You could have
walked away then. You had every right to decide that a man who runs
when things get complicated wasn't worth the risk. Instead, you fought
for us. You made me see that choosing love over fear isn't selfish—it's the
bravest thing we can do."

I pause, including Maddie in my gaze before returning to Annie. "I
promise to love you with the complete commitment you deserve. To
face our challenges together rather than retreating into old patterns of

self-protection. To build a family with you that honors our past while embracing our future."

Looking directly into her eyes, I make the vow that matters most. "I promise to choose love over fear, every day, for the rest of our lives. To love you not despite life's uncertainties, but because of them—because every moment of happiness is precious."

Annie's smile is luminous through her tears as she begins her own vows. "Jake," she says, her voice clear and sure. "Twenty years ago, I thought loving you was part of my past. Five months ago, I thought losing you again might break me. Today, I know that loving you—with all your complications and fears and beautiful heart—is the greatest privilege of my life."

She squeezes my hands tighter. "I promise to be patient when fear whispers lies about our future. To remind you, as often as necessary, that love shared is love multiplied, not divided. To create a home with you where all our family feels safe and cherished."

She glances at Maddie, then returns to me. "I promise to love you through whatever life brings our way—joy and sorrow, triumph and challenge, ordinary Tuesday mornings and extraordinary celebrations. To be your partner, your best friend, your safe harbor in any storm."

Her voice grows more intense with emotion. "And I promise to choose courage over comfort, love over safety, hope over fear—because you taught me that the best things in life are worth the risk."

There isn't a dry eye in the house as Mayor Wilson invites us to exchange rings. The simple platinum bands we've chosen reflect our preference for understated elegance, engraved inside with the date and our shared promise, "Love over fear."

"By the power vested in me by the State of Texas and the town of Firelight Falls," Mayor Wilson declares after the rings are exchanged, "I now pronounce you husband and wife. Jake, you may kiss your bride."

I don't need to be told twice. Drawing Annie into my arms, I kiss her with all the love, gratitude, and promise I feel in this perfect moment. Our assembled friends and family erupt in applause, but I'm only vaguely aware of them, my world narrowed to the woman in my arms—my wife, my Annie, mine again after all these years.

When we finally part, both slightly breathless, Maddie steps forward with something in her hands—a small white candle rather than the traditional unity candle.

"This represents our family," she explains to the gathered guests, her voice clear despite her obvious emotion. "Not just the love between Dad and Annie, but the love that includes all of us—Mom's memory, Grandma Martha and Grandma Rose, all the people who have shaped us into who we are today."

Annie and I each place a hand on the candleholder with Maddie's, the three of us lighting it together as Mayor Wilson concludes the ceremony. "What love has joined, let nothing put asunder. Ladies and gentlemen, I present to you for the first time, Mr. and Mrs. Colton, and their daughter Maddie."

The reception that follows is everything we'd hoped for—joyful, intimate, focused on family and community rather than elaborate traditions. We share our first dance to the same jazz song we'd danced to in Annie's apartment the night we first kissed again, moving together like we were made for each other.

Later, after everyone's eaten, and people are crowding the dance floor around us, Annie looks up at me with an expression of complete contentment.

"Happy?" I ask, though the answer is obvious in her radiant smile.

"Completely," she confirms. "Though also a little amazed that we actually made it here."

"Having second thoughts?" I tease gently.

"Only about how long it took us to figure this out," she says. "But I think maybe we needed those twenty years apart to become the people who could love each other properly."

As we continue to dance, surrounded by the people who love us most, I'm overwhelmed by gratitude for this unexpected life—for the woman who has become my wife against all odds, for the daughter who pushed me toward happiness when I was too afraid to reach for it myself, for the community that has supported our love story from the beginning.

Twenty years ago, I left Firelight Falls believing I was protecting Annie from my complicated life. I see now how wrong I was—how much stronger we are together than apart.

As the evening winds down and we prepare to begin our new life as husband and wife, I whisper what is on my heart, "I'm still yours."

"Always mine," Annie murmurs, her head resting comfortably on my chest.

And this time, I know it's forever.

# *Epilogue*

## Jake

I'VE BEEN THROUGH BURNING buildings, flipped trucks, and once had to pull a very grumpy raccoon out of a chimney. But none of that prepared me for Annie, barefoot on a hotel balcony, wearing one of my old t-shirts and holding two mugs of coffee like she's about to solve world peace with caffeine.

"This view is insane," she says, handing me a mug before curling back up in the lounge chair with a sigh. "I feel like I'm in a postcard."

The view is magnificent. Ocean, sunrise, all that. But honestly? She's the postcard.

And I'm the lucky idiot who gets to keep her forever.

"I still can't believe you wore those socks to our wedding," she adds, eyeing me over her mug.

"They were fire hydrants. They matched the theme."

"They clashed with your dress blues."

"They clashed with your expectations. I think they made a statement."

She shakes her head, but she's smiling. That soft, sleepy smile I've grown to love since our wedding night. Her hair's doing that thing where it curls at the ends when it's humid, and there's a small crumb from the croissant we shared stuck to the corner of her mouth. I reach over and brush it away with my thumb.

"What?" she asks, catching my hand and pressing a kiss to my palm.

"Nothing. Just... you."

We're in Galveston for the weekend—her pick. Fancy bed-and-breakfast. White linens. A tiny bakery down the street that she's already made plans to visit three times. I didn't question it. I'd follow her anywhere, even into a very floral-scented tea shop where I was the only man and the only person over six feet tall.

"You okay?" she asks, reaching for my hand with her free one.

I nod. "Better than okay. I'm sitting next to my wife, drinking coffee, and pretending I don't hear the seagulls arguing over half a waffle down there."

The word 'wife' still catches me off guard sometimes. Three days married, and I keep waiting for someone to tell me it's all a mistake, that I don't actually get to keep her. Twenty years of believing I'd blown my shot don't disappear overnight, even when the woman you love is sitting right next to you wearing your old Houston FD t-shirt and looking completely content.

Annie leans her head against my shoulder. "We should stay forever."

I laugh. "Can't. Chief already texted me asking if I took the firehouse hose arch with me. He's convinced I 'borrowed' it."

She snorts. "You made everyone keep it up for our first kiss."

"Hey, we earned that moment."

The memory makes me grin—our wedding party, half the fire department, and most of Firelight Falls holding those dress uniform axes high while Annie and I kissed underneath them like we were the only two people in the world. Caroline had cried. Maddie had rolled her eyes but smiled the whole time. Even my mother had been lucid enough to clap and call out, "About time!"

A breeze brushes past us, warm and salty and lazy. Annie pulls her knees up into the chair, her ring catching the morning light. I can't stop staring at it. At the reminder that this is real.

She's real.

This whole messy, perfect life is real.

"You ever think about how different things could've turned out?" she asks suddenly, her voice quieter.

"All the time."

"And?"

"And I'd do it all again. Even the hard stuff. Because it brought me back to you."

It's true. The years in Houston, the oil rig work, even losing Lisa—all of it shaped me into someone who could appreciate what I have with Annie. Someone who understands that love isn't guaranteed, that happiness has to be chosen every day, that second chances are rare and precious things.

Annie doesn't say anything for a second, just squeezes my hand and rests her cheek against my arm. I can feel her smile against my shoulder.

"Even the part where you were a complete idiot a few months ago?" she asks.

"Especially that part," I say, pressing a kiss to the top of her head. "Because it taught me you're brave enough to fight for us when I'm too scared to fight for myself."

Her free hand finds the hem of my t-shirt, her fingers tracing small circles on my stomach in that absent way she has when she's thinking. It's become one of my favorite things about being married to her—all these small intimacies, these unconscious touches that say 'you're mine' without words.

"Maddie texted," she says after a moment. "Apparently, Caroline made pancakes this morning and burned them, so they ordered pizza for breakfast."

I shake my head. "My sister can negotiate million-dollar divorces but can't flip a pancake to save her life."

"She's trying. That's what matters."

"True. Though I'm pretty sure Maddie's going to come home with some interesting stories about Aunt Caroline's cooking attempts."

The thought of my daughter bonding with my sister over culinary disasters makes me smile. Caroline had volunteered to stay with Maddie for our long weekend getaway, despite not being able to cook. But she'd been determined to give us time alone, to help cement this new phase of our family.

"Do you miss her?" Annie asks. "Maddie, I mean. I know three days isn't long, but..."

"Yeah," I admit. "But also, no. Does that make sense?"

She turns in her chair to look at me properly. "Explain."

"I miss her because she's my kid, and I'm programmed to worry when she's not within shouting distance. But I don't miss having to share you with anyone else for a few days."

Annie's cheeks pink slightly. "That's very selfish of you, Mr. Colton."

"I'm a selfish man, Mrs. Colton."

The way her eyes light up when I call her that makes my heart feel like it's going to burst from my chest. She's been Annie Barrett for forty-two years, and now she's Annie Colton, and somehow that small change feels like the most significant thing in the world.

"I like the sound of that," she murmurs, leaning forward to kiss me softly. She tastes like coffee and strawberry jam from our earlier croissant, sweet and warm and perfectly Annie.

When we break apart, she settles back in her chair but keeps hold of my hand, our fingers intertwined in a way that's become second nature.

"Can I tell you something?" she asks.

"Always."

"The night I read the letters, I kept thinking about this line you wrote. About me being your true north."

I remember that letter—one of the last ones, written just before I came back to Firelight Falls. I'd been at my lowest point, missing her with an ache that felt physical, wondering if I was crazy to uproot my life on the slim chance she might still feel something for me.

"I meant every word," I tell her.

"I know you did. But, Jake, you need to know—you've been my true north too. All these years. Even when I convinced myself I'd moved on, even when I dated other people, even when I thought you were just a memory... You always felt like home."

"Annie..."

"I used to have this recurring dream," she continues. "I'd be lost somewhere—a forest, a city, a maze—and I'd call your name and somehow, you'd always find me."

Guilt twists in my stomach. "I'm sorry. I'm sorry you carried that for so long."

"Don't be sorry," she says firmly. "Be grateful. We both carried each other through twenty years apart. That's not a burden—that's a miracle."

She's right, of course. Annie's always been better at seeing the bigger picture, at finding the meaning in our pain instead of just wallowing in it.

"So what happens now?" I ask. "We go back to Firelight Falls, I return to pulling cats out of trees, you go back to feeding half the town, and we just... live happily ever after?"

Annie laughs, but there's something wistful in it. "Is that what you want? Happiness?"

"With you? Yes. Absolutely."

"Even if simple gets complicated sometimes? When your mother's health declines more, when Maddie starts dating seriously, when the bakery gets busy, when you have to work double shifts during fire season?"

I consider her question seriously. A year ago, complications felt like threats to be avoided. Now, with Annie beside me, they feel like life—messy and challenging and completely manageable as long as we face them together.

"Especially then," I say. "Because now I know the secret."

"Which is?"

"Complicated problems are easier to solve when you're not trying to solve them alone."

Annie's smile could power the whole hotel. "Look at you, getting all wise in your old age."

"Learned from the best," I tell her, bringing her hand to my lips to kiss her knuckles.

"What will we argue about?" I ask after a while.

"You'll want the thermostat at sixty-eight. I'll want it at seventy-two. You'll leave coffee rings on my grandmother's dining table. I'll rearrange your tools."

"Sounds terrible," I deadpan.

"The worst," she agrees, grinning.

"When do we start?"

"Tomorrow?"

Just like that, we're planning a future together. Not just the big romantic gestures or the milestone moments, but the mundane details that make up a shared life. It should feel overwhelming, but it feels right—like we're finally doing what we should have been doing all along.

My phone buzzes with a text from Maddie.

> Maddie: Caroline tried to make eggs. We're having cereal. Again. Please come home soon before I starve.

I show the message to Annie, who laughs so hard she nearly spills her coffee.

"We should probably rescue her," she says.

"Probably. Though I bet Caroline's learning as much as Maddie is."

Another text comes in.

> Caroline: Your daughter is teaching me to make scrambled eggs. When did fifteen-year-olds become so competent? Also, she wants to know if Annie has a recipe for those chocolate chip muffins because apparently, I can't just buy them from the store like a normal person.

"Your family," Annie says, reading over my shoulder and shaking her head.

"Our family," I correct. "Think you can handle all of us full-time?"

"Bring it on, Colton. I've been handling difficult customers for years."

I set down my coffee mug and lean over to kiss her properly, the kind of kiss that makes her sigh against my mouth and forget whatever witty comeback she was planning. When we break apart, we're both grinning.

And for the first time in twenty years, I'm not afraid of what comes next. Whatever complications await us in Firelight Falls—teenagers and aging parents and businesses to run and a community that likes to keep track of everyone's business—we'll handle them together.

We sit like that for a long time. Just the two of us. No alarms. No paperwork. No bakery ovens beeping.

Just sunrise and coffee and a woman who still somehow loves me, even after I spilled powdered sugar on her wedding dress and wore fire hydrant socks to our ceremony and spent too long being too scared to tell her how I felt.

The luckiest idiot in Texas, finally smart enough to hold on to his happiness with both hands.

Finally home.

• • • • • • • • • •

Thank you for reading *Still Yours, Always Mine*. I hope you enjoyed Jake and Annie's second-chance story as much as I do. If you have a minute, I'd love for you to leave a review.

Want to keep in touch? Join my newsletter and never miss a new release, cover reveal, or update! Plus, you'll get a FREE story, just for signing up! tiamarlee.com/newsletter

Ready for more Firelight Falls? Grab *Catch Me If You Can*, and see if Caroline can outrun her feelings.

# Also By Tia Marlee

**Piney Brook Wishes Series**

*His Christmas Wish*

*Sweet Summertime Wishes*

*Wishing for the Girl Next Door*

*A Soldier's Wish*

*Her New Year's Wish*

*The Piney Brook Wishes Box Set*


**The Coffee Loft Series**

*Bean Wishing for a Latte Love*

*You Mocha Me Crazy*

*A Brewtiful Kind of Love*

Coffee Loft Collection


**Apple Blossom Ranch Series**

*His to Adore*

*His to Have*

*His to Hold*
*His to Love*
*His to Cherish*
*Hers to Treasure*

## Sugar and Sirens
*Still Yours, Always Mine*
*Catch Me, If You Can*
*Sweeter With You*
*A Little Bit Married*
*The Last First Kiss*

## A Cobb County Christmas
*Merry & Bright: The Great Light Fight*
*Gnome Sweet Home*
*The Candy Cane Parade*

# Let's Stay In Touch

You can find me at my website: https://tiamarlee.com

Follow me:

Facebook: https://tinyurl.com/FBTiaMarlee

Instagram: https://tinyurl.com/IGTiaMarlee

Amazon: https://tinyurl.com/AmazonTiaMarlee

BookBub: https://tinyurl.com/BBTiaMarlee

Goodreads: https://tinyurl.com/GRTiaMarlee

Join my reader group: https://tinyurl.com/TiaMarleeReaderGroup

# About Tia

Tia Marlee resides in Central Texas with her husband and three teenage children. When she isn't writing, Tia enjoys reading, embroidery and spending time with her family. Tia is the author of sweet, no-steam, small-town, contemporary romance stories. Her books are like Hallmark meets real life with a dash of humor.

Follow Tia on Facebook, Instagram, or check out her website for more information.